09/09

The Way We Roll

Also by Stephanie Perry Moore

Perry Skky Jr. series

Prime Choice
Pressing Hard
Problem Solved
Prayed Up
Promise Kept

Beta Gamma Pi series

Work What You Got

The Way We Roll

A Beta Gamma Pi Novel
Book 2

Stephanie Perry Moore

KENSINGTON PUBLISHING CORP.

www.kensingtonbooks.com

DAFINA BOOKS are published by

Kensington Publishing Corp.
119 West 40th Street
New York, NY 10018

All Kensington titles, imprints, and distributed lines are available at special quantity discounts for bulk purchases for sales promotion, premiums, fund-raising, educational, or institutional use.

Special book excerpts or customized printings can also be created to fit specific needs. For details, write or phone the office of the Kensington Special Sales Manager: Attn. Special Sales Department. Kensington Publishing Corp., 119 West 40th Street, New York, NY 10018. Phone: 1-800-221-2647.

Dafina and the Dafina logo Reg. U.S. Pat. & TM Off.

ISBN-13: 978-0-7582-3443-8
ISBN-10: 0-7582-3443-0

First Printing: May 2009
10 9 8 7 6 5 4 3 2 1

Printed in the United States of America

For
Marjorie Kimbrough
(My godmother sent from above)

Know that the bond of sisterhood we share
encourages me and helps me
keep on rolling for God!
It is my prayer that every woman experience
such real friendship—no jealousy, no strife . . . just love.
And that every reader know that
she must not only seek real sisters
but be a real sister as well.

ACKNOWLEDGMENTS

Sorority life can be so fulfilling—especially when the sorority members deeply care for one another, come together for a common purpose, and have each other's back. The sisterhood should uplift each member and be a positive experience. Unfortunately I know firsthand that sisters are not always "on the same page." The positive attributes that come from strong-willed women working together can also be a downfall when those strong heads butt against each another. Disaster strikes when people care more about themselves than what is best for the group. Applying the simple biblical truth—to love thy neighbor as thy self—can make the sisterhood bond deep, honest, real, and blessed.

Crafting a story about what sisterhood should really be means a lot to me. In my own organization, I currently am the Southern Regional Membership Services/Sisterhood Chairperson. Trying to find a way to please many people seems impossible. Many times I feel defeated with tasks before I even attempt to begin the job. Thankfully, the Lord has allowed me to believe that as long as my heart wants to serve others, pray for them, and see that only His best happen for them, then I'm truly serving the members. Loving on your sisters is not about pleasing them, it's about wanting to make them happy. I know that if everyone looks inside themselves and steps up the love they have for one another, our world will be a better place. My writing exists only because of those who love me, and to them I give a huge thank-you.

For my family: parents, Dr. Franklin and Shirley Perry, Sr.; brother, Dennis; and sister-in-law, Leslie. For my mother-in-law, Ms. Ann. For my extended family: Bobby and Sarah Lundy, Antonio and Gloria London, Cedric and Nicole Smith, Harry and Nino Colon, Brett and Loni Perriman, Chandra Dixon, and Michele Clark Jenkins—thanks for sharing your *heart* with me. May every friendship feel this good. The tie is real when hearts connect.

For my publisher, Kensington/Dafina Books, and especially my soror, Lesleigh Underwood—thanks for giving your *resources* to me. May every friend always give and share like you do. The bond of friendship will grow when we don't hold on to our assets but rather use them to help someone else.

For my writing team: Carolyn O'Hara, Ashley Duncan, Chantel Morgan, and Alyx Pinkston—thanks for the *effort* you give me. May everyone learn that it takes hard work to be in a true relationship or job of any kind. The bond can be resilient when both parties are in it for the long haul.

For my DST sorors, for whom I care deeply (especially my special sisters): Jenell Clark, Deborah Thomas, Christine Nixon, Cassandra Brown, Sarah Lundy, Isha Western, Pam Murphy, Dayna Fleming, Yolanda Rogers-Hauser,

Anitra Shaw, Cynthia Boyd, and in memory of Brenda Haywood—thanks for the *connection* you share with me. May the compassion for others always be something deeply felt in our organization. The sisterhood bond is tighter when we see a soror as we see ourself.

For my children: Dustyn Leon, Sydni Derek, and Sheldyn Ashli—thanks for the *trust* you place in me. May you know I'm always here for you. The bond is tighter because we are each doing our part to make it work.

For my hubby, Derrick Moore, thanks for the *intimacy* between us. May that flame of love we share never die. The bond is unbreakable because we are one.

For my readers, thanks for the *blessing* your support gives me. May the message in this novel speak to your heart. The bond I feel we have as author and reader is one I hold dear because we're here to make each other's worlds better.

And for my Savior, thanks for the grace You daily grant me. May every person understand that if You can forgive us, we should forgive those who trespass against us. And then may they know the relationship bond is everlasting when forgiveness is attached.

BETA GAMMA PI
TRADITIONS, CUSTOMS, & RITES

Founding Data

Beta Gamma Pi was founded in 1919 on the campus of Western Smith College by five extraordinary women of character and virtue.

Sorority Colors

Sunrise lavender and sunset turquoise are the official colors of Beta Gamma Pi. The colors symbolize the beginning and the end of the swiftly passing day and remind each member to make the most of every moment.

Sorority Pin

Designed in 1919, the pin is made of the Greek letters Beta, Gamma, and Pi. This sterling silver pin is to be worn over the heart on the outermost garment. There are five stones in the Gamma: a ruby representing courageous leadership, a pink tourmaline representing genuine sisterhood, an emerald representing a profound education, a purple amethyst representing deep spirituality, and a blue sapphire representing unending service.

Anytime the pin is worn, members should conduct themselves with dignity and honor.

The B Pin

The B Pin was designed in 1920 by the founders. This basic silver pin in the shape of the letter B symbolizes the beginning step in the membership process. The straight side signifies character. The two curves mean yielding to God and yielding to others. It is given at the Pi Induction Ceremony.

Sorority Flower

The lily is the sorority flower and it denotes the endurance and strength the member will need to be a part of Beta Gamma Pi for a lifetime.

Sorority Stone

The diamond is the sorority stone which embodies the precious and pure heart needed to be a productive member of Beta Gamma Pi.

Sorority Call

Bee-goh-p

Sorority Symbol

The eagle is the symbol of Beta Gamma Pi. It reflects the soaring greatness each member is destined to reach.

Sorority Motto

A sisterhood committed to making the world greater.

The Pi Symbol

The Bee insect is the symbol of the Pi pledges. This symbolizes the soaring tenacity one must possess to become a full member of Beta Gamma Pi.

Contents

BECOMING

If I see one more Beta Gamma Pi girl looking down at me because I'm not sporting any of them pitiful letters, I might just kick her tail. Yes, I'm here at their convention, but I am not Greek. I'm not here like other wannabes; I'm here because I have to be.

My mom, Dr. Monica Jenkins Murray, is their National President, and that makes me sick. I can't believe my time with my mom has taken a backseat to the sorority. For real, when it came to my mom doing sorority business versus my mom being a mom, I came last every time. Yeah, she said all the sorority stuff was for the good of the community and one day I'd understand her sacrifice, but when she didn't make any of my piano recitals or, parent-teacher conferences, I started to detest the group she loved.

After my parents divorced and my older brother moved out with my dad, it was just my mom and me. Though we lived in the same house, we were worlds apart. Basically I felt Beta Gamma Pi took everything away from me. I was at the National Convention only because some of the ladies on the executive board were more of a mom to me than my own mother. The First Vice President, Deborah Day, who lived in California, begged me to come support their endeavors. Because she was always there when I needed someone to talk to, I came. Plus, the VIP rooms in the hotel were stocked with alcohol. With no one around to supervise, I was feeling nice.

"You're all smiles. I guess you just finished kissing the National President's butt, huh?" I said to a girl coming out of my mom's presidential suite.

"I'm sorry, do I know you?" the girl said, squinting, trying to figure out who I was.

"You're so full of it," I said, calling her out as I stumbled, trying to get my key to work on the door. "You know who I am. You're just trying to get on my good side to raise your stock with her."

The girl persisted. "I'm sorry, I'm not trying to offend you, but you really do look familiar. Do you need some help with that?"

I snatched my hand away. "I don't need your help."

"What's going on out here?" The door flung open, and my mom came out in the hallway.

"I was, uh trying to get in the room." I fell back a little.

"Girl, you are so embarrassing me. Get your drunk behind in here now," my mom said sternly. Then she sweetly spoke to the other girl. "Hayden, come in, please."

"Wasn't she just leaving?" I said. I was so confused. My mom went over to this Hayden girl and just started explaining my behavior, like she needed to apologize to some college girl about how I was acting. Why couldn't my mom apologize to me that I had to put up with a brownnoser?

"Come here, Malloy, I want to introduce you guys," my mom said. I reluctantly walked over to them. "Hayden Grant, this is my daughter Malloy Murray. Malloy, Hayden is the Chapter President of Beta Gamma Pi on your campus."

"See, I thought I knew you." The girl smiled, and she reached to shake my hand. "I'm going to be a junior. I knew I'd seen you around school, but I didn't know this was your mom."

"Yeah, sure you didn't know this was my mom," I said sarcastically while keeping my arms glued to my sides.

My mom huffed, "Lord, you don't have to be rude."

"Then don't force me to talk to someone I don't want to talk to, and don't apologize for how I'm feeling. I have a right to be angry, okay, Mom? I don't want to embarrass you anymore, so please get this girl out of my face. I don't care what school she goes to. Unlike both of you, I don't think Beta Gamma Pi is God's gift to the world."

"Hayden, I'm so sorry about this again. Let's just keep this between us. My daughter doesn't usually drink. She'll be much more herself when you guys get back to school. Let's just say I do look forward to working more closely with your chapter, particularly when Malloy makes line."

"Yes, ma'am," Hayden said, really getting on my nerves. She could not get out of the suite fast enough for me. Of course, after she left, my mom looked at me like she was disappointed. Shucks, I was the one rightfully upset. The alcohol just allowed me to finally let out how I felt.

"Mom, don't go making no promises to that girl about me being on line. I'm in school to get an education, not to pledge. Plus, their last line was crazy. They haze up there. You want me to have something to do with that? You're the National President. You're supposed to be against any form of hazing. I'm telling you it was all around school that they put a girl from the last line in the hospital."

She looked at me and rolled her eyes. I believed what I was saying. Some of those girls would do anything to wear Greek letters. Not me.

Changing her tone, she said, "Sweetheart, if you're a part of it, they won't do anything like that. I don't have to worry about anybody doing anything you don't want, as tough as you are. Just promise me you'll take this into consideration. This is one of my hopes for you, Malloy. Being a part of this sisterhood can be so fulfilling. You don't even have a best friend, for crying out loud."

"Yeah, for crying out loud, one of your biggest dreams for me is to be in a sorority. Not to fall in love with a man and stay married forever—like you couldn't. Not to graduate from college with honors and get a great job or doctorate—like you did. Instead, you're praying your child gets into a sorority. I might have had a couple drinks, but it's clear to me that's the thing you want most for me." I plopped down on the couch, picked up the remote, clicked on the television, and put the volume on high. "Don't hold your breath on me becoming a Beta. Sweet dreams, Mommy."

She went into her part of the suite and slammed the door. I knew I had disappointed her. However, as much as she had disappointed me in my life, we weren't anywhere close to being even.

"Mikey," I said the next morning as I came out of my side of the large executive suite I was sharing with my family and saw my brother watching the sports channel with his friend.

"Hey, sis," he said, squinting his eyes as he looked at my outfit.

I hadn't realized my silk gown was open, and the little nightie I wore was revealing much more than my brother wanted his friend to see.

"Cover up, girl. Dang," Mickey said.

"Not on account of me," his friend said with a smirk.

The guy was so fine. I could see the outline of his chiseled chest through the T-shirt he wore. When I looked harder I knew exactly who he was. It was Kade Rollins, the starting linebacker for the University of Southeastern Arkansas.

Mikey was a defensive back on the same team. He wasn't that great, but he'd started. On the contrary, this Rollins guy was great. I remembered the sports writers wondering why he didn't go pro last year. Kade was staying for his senior year to graduate and make his stock go even higher. He was predicted to go in the first round of the draft.

Kade's dark mocha eyes were so into me. I was actually loving the glare. It made me feel sexy. Mikey was furious. I turned around and went back into my room as Mikey followed.

"What's up with that? Why are you going to come out and be all disrespectful like that? Fix your clothes."

"Wait a minute. You came into the place where I'm staying at with mom. Dude, you haven't seen her in, what, a year? And I wake up, and you're here with some friend. Now *I'm* the one being disrespectful because I'm comfortable? Please. I didn't even know you were coming, and the last person I'd expect you to be hanging with would be Kade Rollins. The last few years, you've always dissed the guy. Now y'all hanging out all buddy-buddy and stuff?"

"The guy stayed here for his senior year. Obviously he didn't look out for himself. I misjudged him, okay? Get dressed. The last thing I want him to be doing is looking at my sister. He's a player." Mikey pointed his finger in my face like I had to heed his words or else.

"We haven't lived together in, like, five years. Don't act like you're my dad and stuff. I had to look out for myself. I can do what I want when I want. Move!" I said as I flung open my door and pranced right back out.

"So, Kade, what brings you to the Beta convention? This is a sorority thing. I'm surprised to see you here," I asked, wanting to make my brother madder.

Mikey blurted out, "His girlfriend is here."

"No, no, don't be telling her all that." Kade got up and came toward me. "Mikey, you've been holding out. Your little sister is pretty grown-up to me."

My brother's cell phone rang, and he answered it. Apparently it was my mom. She needed some help setting something up in one of the meeting rooms.

"Why can't she get a bellman to do this stuff? Come on, Kade, will you help me?" my brother said to his boy.

"Oh, man. I'm looking at the game," he said, looking deep into my eyes.

"Malloy, get dressed," Mikey said as he walked out of the suite.

Kade walked over to me. "You don't want to get dressed. What you want to do is get undressed."

"You first," I said to him.

"Oh, you ain't said nothing but a word." He started unbuttoning his shirt.

"Please, I have no interest in looking at a little boy." I turned around and walked back into my bedroom.

"Okay, why are you going to play hard to get with me?"

"Didn't my brother just say you had a girlfriend?" I said through the door as I put on some jeans and a T-shirt.

"Something I'm coming out of, but don't you want to give me something to get into?" he said seductively.

I opened the door, and he almost fell inside the room. "Dang, can a sister get some privacy? What you want to see that bad? You trying to put on your X-ray vision or something?"

"Naw, naw. I just was . . . Okay, you caught me."

I don't know what my mom had Mikey doing, but it lasted about thirty-five minutes, and during that time Kade and I just chatted. He was impressed with how much I knew about football, which wasn't a big deal to me. I was brought up on it; my big brother loved the sport, and my dad did, too. The only way I could get any real attention from my father was when we talked about football. I felt so comfortable chatting with Kade that I confessed how angry I was with my dad. My Dad made me feel like he divorced not only my mom but me as well. Yeah, he gave me money, but he never gave me his time. I resented him for that.

I was shocked when Kade revealed, "Yeah, I understand that. My dad left my mom and me when I was little. Then when I started doing well in high school, he started to come around. He hadn't paid my mom a dime in child support before that, but when I had a chance to make it out of the projects, he was the first one trying to show up, acting like he was some real father. I don't know what kind of baller I'm going to be. I just know when I have a chance to become a father, I'm not going to be one that walks away."

"I've seen you play. You come off that corner like no one else I've ever seen. All that anger and passion you channel toward your opponent—I really understand it. I'm angry about a lot of things, too, Kade, but at least you have an outlet. You have a good way of expressing it, and you're successful at it. Don't worry, just keep your head on straight and keep playing with that fire, and nobody will be able to deny you."

Gazing into my brown eyes, he said, "You're denying me now 'cause you won't go out with me."

"For what, so I can be the new girl of the month and then you can ditch me like you supposedly ditched your girlfriend? I don't think so. And anyway, I just met you."

"You're fiercer than any opponent I've ever seen on the field and definitely more intriguing than any girl I've ever met. You're telling me I'm a great player, but you don't want to get with me. Honestly this has never happened to me before."

"What, I'm not feeding your ego? It is what it is. News flash: you're just a guy."

He came over to me and bent down to my ear. "Just a guy that wants to get with this beautiful girl."

"And you're trying too hard," I said to him as I moved away.

Thankfully the door opened. Mikey was back, and he could tell his boy was way into me. Mikey didn't like it at all. I didn't care. Flirting that went nowhere was fun.

Later that evening, I was at the Beta Gamma Pi Collegiate Stepshow Afterparty. I had been coming to these things for years, and it had always been a big part of the convention. Though only Betas participated in the stepshow, all the fraternities and sororities were in the house. I was used to being alone, but for some reason tonight I felt isolated, and it wasn't as cool of a feeling as it had always been. On either side of me there were clusters of people nestled beside me laughing and having a good time.

The whole sisterhood-friendship-bond thing was something I just didn't understand, but maybe I wanted to. I quickly shrugged that off when Mikey and Kade came walking toward me. Kade had on a buttoned up shirt he'd unbuttoned most of the way. His chest was popping out from behind the shirt, and he was looking superfine.

"You seen any of the Betas from your school?" Mikey asked me.

"No, I don't hang out with them girls," I said real salty 'cause he couldn't even say hello.

"Hey, Mikey." Some girl came over to my brother. "Let's dance, baby."

She pulled him out on the dance floor. There I stood with Kade. Why was I so nervous?

"You look gorgeous tonight."

"I see you're still trying hard," I said, trying to sound uninterested.

"Well, I haven't been able to stop thinking about you all day, and even though I know your brother would probably kill me if I mess with you," he said, licking his lips, "that is just a chance I am willing to take. I'm sprung!"

"You're a liar," I said, completely flustered.

"No, I'm serious."

As I tried to walk away, he grabbed my hand. The touch sent chills up my arm straight to my heart. My heart started beating faster. I knew nothing was gonna happen tonight, but I was willing to go along with Kade. Shoot, the brother was hot.

"You want a drink?" he said.

"Sure, why not."

We walked toward the punch table. When we got there, though, he pulled me over to a doorway past the bartender. I was thirsty and confused.

"Where are we going? The punch is right over there."

"I'm not talking about no punch. I've got a little something in my car. Are you down for that?" He held my hand and gave me a serious stare.

Rolling my eyes, I said, "What, so you could slip me a roofie? I don't think so."

"I don't need to take advantage of you. I just need you to warm up to me. See how hot you can be for me."

I'm a cute girl. Five-nine, slim, nice brown skin, fluffy black hair, and my boobs and butt are in the right place.

I've never had a problem turning a guy's head. But I certainly have never let them know that I was interested, and I certainly didn't give it up on the first date.

So an hour later when we were parked and Kade was on top of me, I was completely shocked. Though this was fast, something real was going on here, and it wasn't just on his side. I wanted him to make me feel good—to heck with being a good girl. When he kissed me, I didn't fight back. When he slid his hand up under my shirt, I didn't move it off. And when his hands went to other places, I felt better than any man had made me feel before. Though I had been with only two guys, they were nowhere close to Kade.

Just when he wanted to get me acquainted with every part of his body, I said, "You know what? I just can't."

"What—doesn't it feel good?"

"You've got a girlfriend. I can't have sex with you."

"I told you that was handled," he said.

"So what—we do this, and then I never see you again? I want more than a fling."

His answer was a passionate kiss. Though he didn't know me, and all this was going way too fast, the brother put it on like he loved me or something. All my fears subsided. I let him have his way with me, and it felt marvelous. Right after, he wanted to hold me, but I just couldn't. Though I had enjoyed it, deep down, another part of me was not really understanding the type of girl I was becoming.

GOSH

I hadn't done anything so crazy and spontaneous ever, but it sure had felt good being with Kade like that. It had been a while since I'd gotten my groove on, and now I felt like a new woman. Stepping back into the crowded stepshow afterparty, I was confident that I had just started something amazing with a guy who had honestly swept me off my feet. I couldn't say it was love at first sight, but it was certainly something close to it.

Or, at least, I thought it was until this girl came rushing over to us and screamed out, "Where have you been, Kade? I told my girls you brought some football players. We were looking all over for you. You tell me you're gonna be here at ten o'clock, I expect you to be here at ten o'clock."

He didn't respond. He just looked down and wouldn't look at me or this chick in the eye. It seemed he didn't want to acknowledge that he and I were together. Yet he didn't want me to know this girl had a claim on him. My brother had been right—obviously Kade was still involved with his girlfriend.

"I thought you said you'd broken up with your girlfriend?" I shouted loudly to him, tired of the silence.

He grabbed my arm and pulled me over to the side. "Why you tryin' to call me out and play me like that in front of Sharon?"

"Oh, that's her name. So that's still your girlfriend? Basically you just played me. What a fool I was!"

"You know I'll handle it. I just got to do it in my own time. I hadn't seen her yet."

"Why'd you make me think you'd already ended it?" I asked, seeing the faith I had in him skate away.

Before we could say anything else to each other, the tired-looking Beta chick with an Alpha chapter jacket came between us. It was just my luck. His girl was a Beta from the college I attended.

"Why is this girl standing around like you're giving her the time of day? She's not even Greek, for crying out loud. I thought she was a Delta or MEM or something. She's a TBD—yes, a To be Determined—and you're sitting there all goo-goo-eyed, embarrassing me. Why'd you make me look all over the place for you, Kade?"

"First of all, you need to quit flinging your little nappy head in my face," I said, pushing her away, as anyone could tell she needed a retouch. "Don't you ever talk to me again. You think just being in a sorority makes you something? Well, it's no big deal, girls wearing letters on a jacket. Don't be so naive. You're so full of yourself, you don't even know how to take care of a man. Now I see why Kade is all over me."

Sharon turned to him and asked, "What is she talking about, Kade? Is there something I need to know here?"

"Wait—I know this girl," a familiar voice said. It was the girl I'd run into in the hall earlier. Hayden came over to me and said, "Can I talk to you for just a second?"

I rolled my eyes and told her, "I'm about to leave."

In a sweeter tone, she said, "No, this'll be really quick. Please."

I looked at Kade with disgust before I turned and walked away. He knew he'd better not ever mess with me again. Sharon was trying to talk to him, but he kept looking at me. He hadn't forced me to go all the way with him, but I should have known better. I got what I deserved.

"What do you want?" I said to Hayden after we'd walked away from Kade and Sharon.

"Why are you so angry, Malloy? When I met you yesterday you were angry at your mom, and now you're giving me an attitude."

"Quit trying to analyze me. I don't need a psych evaluation. I'm getting out of here."

"Look, I don't know what's going on between you and Kade, but that's my line sister Sharon's man."

"And?"

"There's no way you'll ever make line if you keep fooling with him. Sharon's kept girls off line at the University of Southwestern Arkansas, and we don't even go to that school because girls have tried to mess with Kade."

"And you're telling me this because?" I said, not really caring.

"Because your mom is my National President, and I have all but promised her you're going to make line. Don't make it hard for me to do my job. Stay away from him, okay? You can do way better than that guy anyway."

"Are you threatening me, Hayden? Maybe I need to go tell Mommy dearest." I tried to walk away.

"Okay, do what you want. I'm just trying to make this easier for you. You don't have to tell your mom anything. Forget we even had this discussion." she said as I walked away.

When I got up to the presidential suite, I dashed in to my room, slammed the door, fell in the bed, and sobbed. I couldn't remember the last time I'd had a good cry. But I didn't understand how I could have been so wrong about the connection between Kade and I. He'd just been, fronting, playing me like any other honey, trying to get into my pants. And I had always been able to see through guys like that. Kade and I had talked about our fathers; we'd talked about him being broke, and we'd talked about our dreams. We'd talked about a connection that was more powerful than anything either of us had ever felt. I guessed all that had meant nothing.

I punched the pillow as if it were his face. Then suddenly, I felt dirty. I stripped, ran into the bathroom, and showered. I could have stayed in there for an eternity, still never feeling clean enough. But when the hotel water got colder, I was forced to get out and really deal with how I was feeling. A good ten minutes later, I heard the door to the suite open, and my brother and Kade came in laughing.

Mikey said, "Dang, man, you had all the honeys swooning. I can't believe you put her in her place like that."

"You think your sister is here?" Kade asked.

"I don't know."

I couldn't even front like everything that had just happened was no big deal. Kade had lied to me about how he'd felt, and I hated him for that.

I opened my suite door, the bath towel still wrapped around me, and yelled, "Get him out of here now, Mike! He's not welcome here!"

"Girl, why you keep coming out here with no clothes on? Dang, I got company."

"It's not like he hasn't seen it all," I said as I opened the towel and dropped it, clearly out of my mind.

I had shocked even my brother. He quickly picked up the towel, and covered my body with it as he pushed me back inside my room. "Go get dressed."

"No. You get him out of here now."

"He's my friend. He's up here, and he's staying here. Mom said we could. You don't own this place."

Opening the door, I went back into the room and said, "Kade, I can't believe you had the nerve to come in here."

"What is she talking about, man? Why is my sister so upset?" Mikey asked his buddy as I tried to hit Kade. "Malloy, get in there and put on some clothes."

Mikey shoved me really hard back into my room, and I hit the dresser. I fell to the floor, and tears filled my eyes.

Mikey shut the door and said, "Malloy, I'm sorry. Are you okay? I didn't mean to push you that hard."

Kade pounded on the door. "You gotta let me in there to see her."

"Man, my sister ain't got on no clothes. Why you tripping?" Mikey stood abruptly as though a revelation had come to his mind. He opened the door. "But why is she so comfortable without clothes in front of you? I told you not to mess with her. I know you ain't crossed that line, Kade, for real."

"You don't understand, man. Your sister's changed me."

"Are you kidding, dude? I just saw you down there in the midst of a whole bunch of honeys. When I couldn't find you at the party, it was because you'd left with my sister?"

"I can explain."

"Naw, partner. And now she in there with a broken heart, and all because you couldn't keep your word. My sister is not easy, and, you like girls that fall all over you. Was she a challenge or something?"

"Naw, naw, I—I—I'll explain it to you later. I just want to talk to Malloy right now."

I put on a robe and walked into their room. "Look, I don't want to talk to you. I told you that downstairs, and I still mean that right now.

"I'm sorry, Mikey. I should have listened to you. He played me just like you said he would. As soon as we got back to the party, he went back to the girl he told me he'd broke it off with."

Trying to defend my honor, my brother jumped on his friend. The two of them started fighting around the room. Kade wasn't even hitting back, though. He was just taking the punches my brother was throwing.

"All right, man," Kade said as blood rushed from his nose. "Malloy, I didn't mean for it to go—"

"Psh, please save it," I said, not even bothering to let him finish.

Kade held up his head and said, "Mike, man, I didn't mean to—"

"Man, please. I don't know how you gon' get back to campus, but you better go try to make up with Sharon or something. I'm through. I asked you to leave Malloy alone, and as soon as I turned my back, you took advantage of her. Dang, man, I hope y'all wore protection."

"Yeah, I was stupid for getting with him in the first place, but I'm not an idiot." I went over to the suite door and opened it.

"I just want to say something. I need to explain. You gotta listen," Kade pleaded.

"Oh, whatever," I said as I shoved him out and slammed the door. Actions speak louder than words. I was done with him.

A couple weeks later, I was home for summer break experiencing the most boring time I'd ever had. I didn't have a girlfriend to call up and go hang out with. There was no guy in my life I could go on a date with. My mom was so involved debriefing the details on the Beta convention, if I wanted a life, I needed to get a job.

I love fashion, and one day I want to run my own clothing line. I have sketch pads full of my thoughts from when I was ten. My mom thought it was a dream job—something that might happen—but she wanted me to do something more stable, like a doctor, teacher, or an administrator like her.

Maybe that was part of our struggle. I wanted her to see my talent and push me, believe in me, and tell me that I could do what I wanted. But all she kept doing was pointing me in other directions. So we compromised. I had wanted to go to design school, but I ended up going to Western Smith College and majoring in business; she hoped I'd become a banker. But I knew I could get the necessary tools to make me successful once I got one of my designs in the right hands.

The only summer job I could find related to fashion was working with the buyers at Wal-Mart. My dad, Michael Sr., was a VP there, and he pulled some strings to work with the buyers. Even though he and I weren't that close, and I had no worries for money because he sent more than I needed, it felt good that he'd hooked me up with a job. Maybe he really did want his baby girl to be truly happy.

Ms. Beverly, the buyer I worked for, was so sweet. Every time sketches came in, I would take my pen and alter them. I always thought my tweaks made them look better.

I didn't know she thought the same thing. "Gosh, girl, you are so talented. I just hate we gotta go to these established companies to get items. When you get that degree behind you, I'll definitely send your stuff over to some of my designer friends in New York. You've got talent!"

I just wrapped my arms around her, which was so uncharacteristic of me. It was hard for me to show emotion. I never cared what anybody else thought, but hearing her say I was good meant something.

When I got home that day, I wanted to make dinner for my mom. I was in such a good mood. She and I hadn't spent any time together, and pretty soon I'd be going back to school. I had the kitchen smelling like we were in Italy with the Italian sauce I'd hooked up, but when she came in, she just started complaining.

"Could you have picked up anything, Malloy? I mean, the same clothes that were sitting on this couch when I left still need to be folded. I didn't ask you to cook for me. I'd rather you just do what I asked you to do. Nothing extra. Just what I asked. You think you can handle that?" she said sarcastically as she left the kitchen.

I couldn't win with her. I was salty. It angered me further when she came back in to get a glass of water.

"You know what, Mom? Let's just be real with each other. Is me pledging the only thing that will make you happy?"

"What, you're considering it?" Her tone immediately changed for the better. "You want to talk to me about what's involved? Yeah. Let's sit—have dinner and talk about it."

"Mom, why does it have to be on your terms? I just wanted to cook you a good meal with no strings attached. I'm your daughter. You're supposed to love me unconditionally, not only in the event that I become a member of Beta Gamma—ugh!" I tossed a hot pan in the sink, splattering the contents, and went toward the doorway.

"No, you come back here and you show me some respect. If you want to talk about this—why I'm so passionate about my desires and the things that I want for you—then you listen fully. Not halfway."

Walking back toward her, I said, "Okay. Shoot, Mom. What? Goodness gracious, spit it out."

"That's just it, Malloy. You're a lovely girl with such potential, but you are so unpolished."

"Mom, if you would have been home when I was younger, teaching me how to hold a cup in my hand when drinking tea, instead of out with some débutantes, maybe I would have more etiquette. I don't think it's my fault."

"In addition to our sorority's five core issues—leadership, sisterhood, education, Christianity, and public service—we believe in poise as well," she said as if I didn't know anything about the organization she loved. "I know that some things a mom just can't teach a daughter. There's this wall between us now that I can't seem to break through. Beta Gamma Pi is all about love, and you definitely need to learn how to let people in. You think you're big and bad and that you know everything, but, sweetheart, I know how broken you are. I hear you crying some nights, and my heart keeps breaking because I can't fix this for you. I strongly believe the sorority will fill a void. All across the country, they're letting girls into the sorority with half your passion, charisma, intellect, and drive."

I couldn't believe it. My mom was giving me compliments.

"And as much as I love my sorority, I know how much it can be changed and made even better. If you channel all that's in you for the right reason, and you find a purpose, you, too, can be better. Though you're my child, Malloy, you're way stronger than me, and you love harder than me. Beta Gamma Pi needs that. Why can't you just give it a try?"

PERIOD

It was the third of July, the day of my twentieth birthday. I was actually looking forward to it. It was the first time in a long time my mother had planned to spend the whole day with me. And because we'd had so much tension between us over the last few years, and I'd be headed back to college soon, I guess she realized it was really now or never. We needed to get our relationship together, or we'd probably always be distant. And though I thought her first love had always been the sorority, she desperately wanted to prove me wrong.

"Mom, I'm ready," I said when I entered her office with an overnight bag. We were supposed to be headed to a spa and then staying overnight at a bed-and-breakfast in Conway, Arkansas. I couldn't wait to be pampered and to really get to know my mom. But she wasn't getting up from her desk. She didn't have the urgency in her voice that I had—she didn't seem excited like me. It didn't take me long to figure out that our plans were off.

"What's going on, Mom?" I asked, trying not to get angry. She finally stood up from behind her big mahogany desk—which was covered with papers with the Beta Gamma Pi emblem on them. It was a good thing her divorce settlement papers paid her enough to sit on her behind. She certainly didn't have time to hold down a real job and simultaneously take care of the Betas' every beck and call.

"What is it now, Mom? You got to do something for them Betas?"

She tried to put her hands on my face. "Oh, sweetie, I need you to understand. I still want to spend time with you, but we've got a problem with the hotel and the conference center from the National Convention. They're threatening to sue us, and I need to take care of this right away with the other officers."

"Mom, I don't understand, and I'm not going to let you off the hook like today didn't matter to me. But do what you got to do. It's not like if I say, 'Don't go,' you're going to celebrate my birthday with me anyway. So what does it matter?" I tried walking away from her, but she latched on to my pinkie and slid closer to me.

"Sweetheart, you got to understand I love you so much. It's just a big responsibility being the National President of an organization."

"It's always politics and business with you, Mom. I used to think family mattered in your life, but now I guess today I'm older, wiser, and can clearly see family is nowhere on your radar. We had plans that you made! Now instead of settling everything with a conference call, you have to go in person and meet with people and put on your charm. Well, try to win them over, because you know what? You've lost me for good."

I knew I was speaking from a place of hurt feelings. I knew I cared too much to cut her out of my life for good. So when I stepped into the hallway, I was surprised that she followed me. My mom always let me have my own tantrums and go my own way. She never really bothered me. But this time was different. This time I was shocked when she said, "I've made arrangements for your brother to come pick you up. He should be here any minute. You two are going to go instead. I know ya'll hit a rough patch at the convention. I don't know what went on or what went down, but ya'll need to fix it. He's up for that, and I need for you to be, too."

Actually intrigued, I said, "Mikey is coming here to take me to some resort?"

"Well, he might have different plans, but he says you're going to love it." She took my hand and laid five one-hundred-dollar bills in it. Of course I smiled.

"And, no, I'm not trying to buy your love," she said. "But I do want you to know that I care about my baby, and I'm so sorry some of my other responsibilities get in the way of things we've planned. I do want to be with you, or I wouldn't have set all this up. And some way, some how the Lord is going to allow me to make it up to you. I promise."

"The Lord? Mom, when is the last time you've been to church? Come on, be real."

"You don't have to go to church to believe. Dang it,

now. Quit being so sassy with me, trying to tell me how I feel and what I want."

"I know you don't want to be with me, or you wouldn't be going somewhere else."

"We just went through this, Malloy. You are twenty years old now, for goodness sake. I don't want to dismiss what you're feeling, but I can't let it dictate how I deal with things that are more important. So go blow the money and have a happy birthday and a good time with your brother. Just please know that I love you. Don't overanalyze anything else. Simply enjoy it all. End of discussion."

"Come on, Malloy, now, you got to admit this shopping spree on Mom's dime is the best," Mikey said as we went from one store to the other, loading up the credit card Mom had given him. I didn't even have to touch the five hundred.

"And she didn't give you a limit?" I asked, my hands full of shopping bags.

"Well, I called, and the card has a ten-thousand-dollar limit. We've spent only one."

"Mikey, have you lost your mind?"

"Naw, I just want my sister to have a happy birthday."

"Okay, what do you want? And why are you acting so weird? Besides you getting a new wardrobe, what's the real reason you took me out?"

"Naw, naw, I'm hanging out with you 'cause I miss my sister. I want you to come hang out with me for a couple days. You'll dig my place. Athletes get to have our own places up at the University during the summer. And I'll sleep on the couch while you take the bed. It'll be like old times. We'll have a ball, for real. Let me show you how I'm rollin'."

My brother had been so busy with football and living a life that had nothing to do with me, this didn't make any sense. He never wanted to hang out with me. Why had that changed? I'd had plenty of birthdays without him, and he hadn't even given me so much as a card.

When we got to Mikey's place, there was a lot of noise coming from the front door. "Mikey, what's going on here? I thought we were going to relax, hang out, pop some popcorn, and chill," I asked.

"We're older now. We should have a little fun. I'm having a party in your honor."

"A party in my honor? I don't know none of your friends." And before I could say, "I do not want to see Kade Rollins," my brother opened the door, and the first person that said happy birthday was Kade.

"Oh, uh-uh," I said as I turned around and walked back out. I didn't even have my car up there, but I knew I wasn't staying in any confined place to allow Kade a chance to tell me more lies.

"Where you going?" My brother said behind me.

"You could have told me. I'm too old for childish, manipulative games, Mikey. Plus, you don't like Kade anymore, or a least I thought that was the way ya'll ended things."

"That was over a month ago. Besides, we're teammates, girl. He crossed the line, but he explained to me that he really does care for you."

"Are you kidding me? And you believe him? You're the one that told me what a big player he was. He humiliated me. I'm not going down that road again."

"Hey, birthday girl!" Some girl headed toward Mikey's place handed me a big present. Then some big guys lifted me up. I was carried into my brother's apartment. This was over the top.

"Put me down! Now!" I demanded.

"Malloy, those are some of my teammates. Everybody is coming to celebrate your birthday. You can't leave."

"We like any reason to party here," said the girl who had handed me a present.

More girls wearing Beta Gamma Pi jackets came in and handed me more gifts. I didn't understand what was happening.

"I'm Jackie," said the first girl with the present. "Don't look confused. These are all for you." Jackie leaned closer. "See, there's two reasons why we got to give you presents, girl. Your mom's the National President, and your brother is hot."

"You guys didn't have to get me anything. Naw, I can't accept these."

"Open mine."

"No, I don't want anything. Thank you." I set them all on the floor. I didn't know my way around this place, but I found a bathroom and shut the door. I just wanted peace. Mikey had gotten me good.

"Hey, ya'll, it's getting too crowded here! We got to move the party to the clubhouse!" my brother screamed out. I heard everyone tearing out of the door, and I was so excited. Finally I'd be alone. After about ten minutes, I opened the door, and standing right before me was Kade. Before I could shut it again, he put his foot in the door.

"Malloy, please. I really want to talk to you."

"And can't you see I don't want to talk to you? You've called me a bunch of times. I didn't know how you got my number, but now I see you and my brother are cool again. You had your little fling, played your little game, but all that is over and done with. Kade, I really don't want to hear anything else you have to say."

"I just can't stop thinking about you, Malloy. Even when I'm supposed to be practicing football, thoughts of you come in and distract me. I can't seem to shake the fact that you're angry with me."

"So this is all about your ego? That I turned you down? Maybe I just didn't end it the right way." I took my hands, grabbed his face, and kissed him without thought. "Now maybe *that's* a proper way to say good-bye. We're finished."

I pushed him out of the way and walked out the front door. I needed to find my brother so I could leave so I followed the signs and walked toward the clubhouse. There was nothing Kade could ever do to get my attention again, and I meant that.

As soon as I walked into the clubhouse, Kade came rushing up behind me and grabbed my arm. I yanked it away and said, "Leave me alone."

"Kade, there you are," Sharon said, appearing out of nowhere with her posse of other Betas from my school.

Sharon looked me up and down. I didn't crack a smile, and neither did she. I didn't know if they thought I was supposed to bow down to them or what. She actually looked surprised when the Betas—from the University of Southeastern Arkansas—came over to me and ushered me onto the dance floor.

"It's your birthday! Let's have a party!" They all lined up and started bebopping all over the place.

Jackie chanted, "Ain't no party like a BGP party 'cause a BGP party really rocks. So come on, get your swerve on, and let your body drop."

All the other Betas screamed, "Beta Gamma Pi in the house!"

"I need to go sit," I said to Jackie, trying to get out of their circle.

The University of Southeastern Arkansas Betas saw the cold stares I was getting from the Western Smith College girls. "I'm Tanya, Vice President of the U of A Kappa chapter, and I wish you went to school here. Obviously our sorority sisters from Alpha chapter don't know how to take care of royalty."

Huffing, I said, "I don't want you kissing my but 'cause my mom is big-time in your organization or whatever."

Tanya said, "It's not just that. You snagged the king."

"What are you talking about?"

"The only thing Kade has been talking about all summer is you. Mikey's little sister this, Mikey's little sister that. Don't you know how many girls here want him? Just look at how many girls are looking over there at him now. And my snooty sorority sister Sharon is desperately trying to hold on to what's obviously over."

"And you think I want to get with him so I could be the flavor of the week? No, been there, done that. Uh-uh."

"I don't know, though. Whatever you did to him, he

hasn't forgotten. He and I have been friends for a long time. I went to high school with both of them."

"Sharon, too?"

"Yeah, we go way back. Her mom is my soror, too. They got a lil' money. My mom isn't a Beta."

"That's a good thing, if you ask me."

"I used to think so. Pros and cons on both sides. Her mom always looked down on me 'cause my mom wasn't Greek. It's weird, but Sharon's a snob, and they ain't that rich. That's why she wants the kind of money Kade's gonna make. She doesn't deserve Kade. He's such a cool guy."

"Well, sounds like you need to date him."

"Naw, he's like a brother to me. We both came from the wrong side of the tracks. He's finally got his chance to soar and fly. He needs somebody like you to take him higher."

"Are you kidding me? You don't even know me, girl."

"Hey, Tanya, we're about to do our step." Hayden came over, a little aggravated that Tanya was giving me so much time.

"I'm talking right now, Hayden. Y'all can wait a second."

Hayden pushed. "We got to get back on the road."

"Cool, do it without me. Jackie's out there, and I'm talking."

Hayden huffed and walked away. She joined the other Betas, and they did more chants. I knew I wasn't winning brownie points with any of them, because every time one passed by, they rolled their eyes at me.

"All right, now. If looks tell it all, seems like it's gonna be very hard for you to make line, girl," Tanya said, keeping it real with me.

"Yeah, I know. It's the one thing my mom wants from me more than anything. I don't think I'll be able to give it to her."

"Just be you and it'll work out. They didn't want me either, but I'm here, working my tail off for the community."

"I don't understand, Kade! I don't get your choice! What does she have that I don't have?" I heard Sharon scream when the DJ stopped the music.

"I'm just saying it's over, all right, Sharon? Why are you trying to control me? I don't want no scene here. You can't keep telling people we're still together when we been broken up," Kade said as she grabbed him.

He got Sharon off him and then gathered the rest of his teammates and left the scene. I knew then that the chick was way desperate. I wouldn't put anything past her.

Sharon rushed up to me. "I hate you. I can't believe he's leaving me for you. You're so full of yourself, and you're just a dang ole' sophomore. You met him, what, a month ago? I've known him for years. I've invested all my time in him. I've given him everything, and he's just gona dump me, talking about he wants to be with you."

"Wait a minute, don't come over here making accusations and putting your finger all in my face. You don't have anything I want. Your sorority or your ex."

"I wouldn't go telling people you don't want to pledge when you know that's what you want to do," Tanya whispered behind me.

"What my mom wants for me and what I want for myself are two different things."

"Oh, that's good," Sharon said as she shoved me and got in my face, "'cause you will never wear these letters. Don't come to the rush! Don't turn in a packet! And do not show up to none of our functions on campus! I don't want to see you anywhere near Beta Gamma Pi stuff. You've been blackballed. You are not wanted, period."

BECAUSE

"Mom, why do you insist on coming with me to move in?" I said, as my mom put her purse in my car the day I was heading back to school. "You said you were gonna come have lunch with me at work, and you never did. Fashion is my heart, and you keep dismissing that. A mom is supposed to support her child in all things. I can go to school alone."

"Because, Malloy, I was tied up all summer. I couldn't come to see your work, but I want to make up for that. The time has gone by, and I know I've been extremely busy with sorority stuff, but I'm not letting you go back to Western Smith alone. Why do you ask anyway, honey? You don't want me to go?"

Her question caught me off guard. It's not like I'm a person who lies. I always shoot straight from the hip, but

I'm not evil, and I didn't want to hurt her feelings. For some strange reason this seemed like it meant a lot to her.

As she put my last suitcase in the trunk, I touched her hand and said, "I'm just surprised at all this. Oh, wait, my laptop is in there."

She moved her hand in circles. "Well, hurry up. We need to get on up there."

"Mom, we're not in a rush. I don't have any classes until next week."

"We are on a time schedule, dear. I have some plans for us, so let's go."

I had no idea what she meant. She had planned something. Maybe she was trying to make up for time missed.

Before I got to my apartment, we stopped at an exquisite restaurant.

"No Mom, I'm not hungry right now. I really want to get settled in my place."

"We have time for that. And of course you're hungry, darling. It's lunchtime. You must eat a little something," she said, being the overprotective mom I knew her to be. "Oh, stop looking so grim. It's not like you're eating with me alone. We'll have someone to stir the conversation," she said, seeing the frown plastered on my face. "And, yes, before you lose it, it is one of my sorority sisters coming to have lunch with us, because then she's going to take me back home."

"So it wasn't really that you wanted to help me move in?" I asked condescendingly. "I mean, we haven't even gone to my place to empty out any of my stuff, and you're saying after we eat you've got a sorority meeting."

"Darling, you said yourself you can handle it. I just wanted to come up here with you. I'm not arguing with you, dear, and if it's that big a deal to you, we can go by the apartment before the meeting, okay?"

"With some lady I don't even know. No thank you," I said, and then there was a knock on the car window.

"Hello!" my mom said in an excited tone.

I looked over and was surprised to see Hayden Grant, standing there like she had an appointment with my mom or something.

"Come on, honey, let's get out. Our lunch date is here."

My mom had to be joking. I didn't want to speak to that girl, much less break bread with her. As we walked to the restaurant, Hayden was so fake with me. I stepped back, giving the two of them space. They chatted and caught up. Watching them interact, it seemed as if my mother was her mother or something. They seemed so friendly and close. Of course as soon as we sat down, my mom got up to go powder her nose, leaving Hayden and me alone.

"Okay, now look," she said to me in a snide tone, "I know you don't want me here."

"So why'd you come?"

"Because your mom asked me to."

"So you came to kiss butt?"

"You need to change your attitude. Keep being so snide and you won't go far in life. You seem so bitter and angry. I know what I need to do to get where I need to go."

"If kissing other people's behinds is going to take you to the next level, maybe we're trying to rise up different buildings."

She just rolled her eyes at me.

"I see you two are chatting away," my mom said as she sat back down. "Very, very good. Let's have a quick lunch, Hayden, so we can help Malloy settle in. We'll have a few minutes before the meeting. I hope that's all right."

"Yes, ma'am, it's fine," Hayden said. "I'd love to help your daughter in any way I can." She displayed another fake grin.

"So I talked to the regional coordinator, and I know you guys are planning to have a line this fall for sure," my mom said as I tried to seem uninterested by keeping my head firmly planted in the menu. "I know Malloy isn't quite sure if she's going to pledge—of course this is hard for me—but I certainly want her to meet your chapter sorority sisters."

"Oh, Mom, I've already met them," I said as I heard Hayden nervously fidget with her plate.

The look in Hayden's eyes was one of panic. She knew I was aware that the Betas had already been talking to the girls they wanted to put on line and that one of her line sisters had came out and point blank told me I'd never pledge Alpha chapter. For some weird reason, I didn't tell this to my mom. Instead I said, "They're cool. They got passion."

"See, I knew you would like these girls." She leaned over and gave me a big hug.

I didn't look at Hayden for her reaction.

Walking to my car two hours later, I said, "Mom, you guys go on to your meeting. I'll be fine."

"You sure, honey? Our meals took longer than I thought."

"I'm fine."

Hayden was walking toward me, but I walked away, got in my car, and drove off. Looking in the rearview mirror, a part of me longed to have the kind of interaction Hayden was experiencing with my mom. Maybe Beta Gamma Pi was the key.

I had just come from the front office and had gotten the keys to my brand-new place. I was so excited not to be in a dorm, to have my own apartment, to live the college life. My new car was loaded down from the backseat to the trunk. While unloading, I resented the fact that my mom wasn't there to help me move in. *I certainly could have used the extra hands,* I thought as I struggled to figure out what to take out first.

I decided to go into the apartment and look around first. Though I had seen the place before I'd left last semester, it was like a breath of fresh air being in my new home away from my mom. Even though we each had our own space, it was still stuffy. However, the newness of this two-bedroom apartment and the possibilities that could lie therein excited me. As I went toward my apartment door to go back to my car outside, I was startled when a hard-looking girl exactly my height suddenly had my door key in her hand.

"You shouldn't leave this in your door, you know."

Quickly I snatched it. Who'd she think she was? And why was she not leaving my space?

"Yeah, thanks. I know."

Her eyes roamed my body. I didn't know if I'd done

something wrong, but I had work to do. I did not have time to stand there with her.

"Um, thanks, I assume you live here?" I asked.

"I'm right next door. Our apartments are joined. I can practically see and hear everything you do. Isn't that great?" she said with way too much excitement.

"Um, yeah, I guess," I said, not wanting to offend her. "I'm Malloy."

"Sirena Rice," she said as she held out her hand to shake mine.

"Oh, I'm dirty. Moving, you know."

"Oh, no problem." She grabbed my hand anyway and firmly shook it up and down.

"Well, thanks for telling me about the key and all," I said, trying to get her to leave.

"You need some help moving?" Sirena asked as she followed me out to my car.

"No, no, thank you."

I did need help, but I didn't know her. What I could size up in two minutes wasn't appealing. The chick was pushy. I didn't need a second mom away from home, but even as I said no, she picked up a box, and inside we headed.

"I'm a senior here. What year are you?" she asked later as we took the second load inside.

"I'll be a sophomore."

She started looking through some of the boxes we'd brought in. Was she loony, or did she simply have no home training? I knew everyone in the world didn't have a mom that lived and breathed from the etiquette book.

Giving her the benefit of the doubt, I set down the box

in my arms and grabbed the one she had. "Thanks, I can get it from here."

"Ah, naw, I'm not trying to be nosy or anything. I just didn't see any paraphernalia, any cheerleading stuff—no dance outfits."

"No, I'm not a part of that."

"Cool," Sirena said. "That stuff can mess up a girl's mind."

Even though I'd told her I didn't need any more help, she refused to stop until everything was inside, organized, and in its right place. We were on a roll. My place was looking good.

"I'm going to have to keep you around. We got through all this today. I wasn't planning on finishing unpacking until the end of the week."

"Organization is key for me."

"What do I owe you? I can't believe you helped me like this," I said, going over to my purse.

"No, I don't want your money. Maybe you could—"

Before she could finish, someone was knocking on my door.

"You expecting somebody?" she asked in a disappointed tone.

"Naw."

"I'll tell them to leave," she said, heading for the door.

I walked around her; I needed to get my own door. I was taken aback when I saw a familiar face. *Oh, no, she isn't at my door.*

It was Hayden Grant, now out of her dressier clothes. The Alpha chapter President was representing as she sported her Beta Gamma Pi T-shirt.

"Can I come in for just a second?" she asked in a sweet tone.

Not buying the nice act, I asked, "How do you know where I live?"

"Your mom told me the apartment address. I have some stuff from her to give you. I saw your car, so I knew you were in. So, here I am."

Seeing my next-door neighbor looking over my shoulder, I didn't want to be rude, so I introduced them. "Hayden, this is Sirena. Sirena, this is Hayden."

"I thought you told me you weren't a part of a sorority," Sirena said, not shaking Hayden's extended hand.

"I'm not!" I said quickly. "But obviously she needs to talk to me about stuff, so thanks for coming over and helping."

Sirena pushed. "Malloy, I can wait until you guys are done. We still have—"

Squinting my eyes to try not to get irritated, I interrupted. "We've done everything. Thank you."

I didn't want to shove her out the door, but she had overstayed her welcome. Thankfully she walked out.

"Sounds like your neighbor is bored or something," Hayden said.

"She's cool. What is it my mama wanted to give me?"

"I don't know. It's this envelope. I didn't open it. Here."

It was certainly my mom's handwriting. What was this letter about? Last year when I was a freshman, she hadn't given me a note.

"You didn't have to take her back home?"

"Naw, she rode with the regional coordinator."

"Oh, I can see them gabbing the entire ride back. Well,

thanks, you gave it to me," I said as I went to open the door again.

"I just wanted to say," Hayden began, "I appreciated you earlier today. You could have told your mom my chapter sorors have been pretty ugly to you, me included. I don't know why you didn't go there."

"Yeah, me neither."

"But I appreciate it, and it shows you got something that maybe we really do need to take a look at. Kade told Sharon you won't see him anymore. So with all that over, I just wanted to let you know that if you'd consider pledging, I want to get you on line."

"Why?"

She shrugged her shoulders, smiled, opened the door, waved, and was gone. I tore open the letter. My mom had written, in big letters, that she loved me. She'd also written that, she prayed I became Hayden's soror. I sat on my bed and reflected on Hayden's last words. I had my chance to please my mom. What was I going to do with it? Honestly I had no clue.

I had been in my apartment for three days. Sirena had been over to my apartment every single day, multiple times, asking to have dinner. I wasn't trying to stay to myself, and I certainly could have used a friend, but I just wasn't bothering with her. She was more than strong-willed, she was overly aggressive. Each time I said no, I knew I had upset her, and I just didn't need to start a friendship with anybody who was that disappointed, when I couldn't spend time with them.

Later that night, my doorbell rang again, and it was her. I almost wanted to scream. I was beyond frustrated. Didn't she get the point? I just wanted to hang out by myself. I needed to relax. I didn't want to talk about anything. A part of me was still dealing with my feelings for Kade. Though I'd tried to push him out of my mind for the past couple months, I'd turn on the TV and, bam, he'd be there, ranked as the state's number-one defensive football athlete. When he was interviewed I could see by his demeanor and his eyes that he really wasn't happy, and I knew it wasn't about him not being with me, he just seemed tired of all the press. I contemplated calling him.

At my door, Sirena said, "Give me one reason why we can't go out for a bite. You say you don't have a boyfriend. You said you're not in any groups or anything. Your car is always here. If it's money, don't worry, I'm taking you out."

I hated to burst her bubble, but money was something I didn't need. My dad sent me a monthly check, and every month I had so much money left over my bank account was ridiculous.

I started holding back my smile when I saw Kade walking up my steps. Sirena couldn't see him because she was looking directly at me.

"Good, so you're going to go. It's not like you have any other plans tonight. Perfect."

"No, she actually does have plans," the husky and warm voice said behind her.

She turned. "Who is this guy?"

I didn't want to say he was a boyfriend, because he certainly wasn't that. I didn't even know if I could call him my friend because last time we'd parted ways I'd told him I didn't want to see him again.

"He's my brother's friend," I said, as if I had no interest.

"Oh? Where's your brother?" She looked around Kade.

Kade looked at her, shrugged his shoulders, and asked if he could come in.

"Sirena, I'll see you later, okay?"

"You gonna talk to him? You gonna go out with this guy, but I been asking you to hang out for days?"

I whispered, "Maybe another time, all right?"

I grabbed Kade's hand, pulled him inside, and shut the door.

He teased, "That girl is creepy."

"She's harmless. What are you doing here? You're the creepy one, showing up unannounced."

"I twisted your brother's arm, and he told me where you live."

"Okay, now you know. Now you see me. Now you can go."

"Come on, Malloy, please don't be like that," he said as he came over to me and pulled out a small box with a bow around it. "I just want to tell you I haven't been able to get over you. I care for you so much, and when I'm out there on the football field, all I keep thinking about is you. I know I dogged you out. . . ."

"Kade, I can't hear any of this, I . . ." But before I could finish, he pulled me to him and kissed me passionately. His tongue and his lips felt so good.

He pulled away and said, "There is no more sharing. I want it to be only you. Can we try?"

"Do you really like me that much?" I asked, and he nodded. "Why?"

He held me so close, and it felt so right. My heart started racing when he said, "Just because."

GUT

"**I** can't seem to shake the thought of you, Malloy. And I wish I could tell you in person how my dream went that had you in it," Kade said into the receiver.

"Oh, see, now you are a hot mess," I said to the phone, as I rolled around in my covers, wishing he were beside me.

We'd been dating for a couple weeks, and most of it had been over the phone because of his intense football schedule and the start of school for me. But I was getting to know him pretty well. Although he had told me several times how special I was to him, I never said it back, and I had a feeling I was starting to fall hard for him. I would be devastated if he hurt me again.

"Okay, so you're quiet, Malloy. What's up today? You know I believe you can accomplish anything."

"Look at you, being a great boyfriend. I'm cool. How was football practice today?"

"It's good, just more intense with our first big game this weekend."

"You'll do fine, and I'll be there with my folks, cheering Mikey on."

"Oh, so you're just coming up to see Mike play?" he asked in an offended tone.

Playing with him, I said, "Well, you didn't invite me."

"I thought that was understood. Of course I'd want my girl there."

Seriously, I said, "I'm not trying to come to this game and have all these other women come out of nowhere claiming you're theirs. Been there, done that, Kade. I'm not trying to put any pressure on you."

"I'm a show-off. I like playing for an audience, and I especially like showing off if my girl is in the stands. Plus, I played that other game before with you and lost once. Not making that mistake again, baby. I just need you here. Besides, I want to see you after the game. The team will throw a big party. We'll get a victory. Then you'll see—I'm going to let the world know you're mine."

He was saying all the right things. Our relationship was under wraps, and I was trying to trust him. He said he trusted me as well, which made me glad he recognized he wasn't the only dude I could put on lockdown.

"Okay, so you're quiet again. What's going on with you, Malloy?"

"I'm just speechless. You're acting too right. And the Beta Gamma Pi rush is tonight. I'm just debating whether or not I even need to show up."

"Sharon, hasn't been messing with you, has she?" he asked.

"Actually, since school started I haven't seen her. Hayden, the chapter president, has been real cool. My mom certainly wants me to do it, but I don't know if it will be the right thing for me. I can do without this entire headache. I don't really have a feeling either way of which way to go."

He urged, "So go to the rush. You won't know what's for you unless you try."

"You think?"

"Yes, and if them girls get on your nerves, just leave and think of me. We can start our own greek organization and call it Me Phi You."

"You are so silly," I told him, really appreciating that he knew how to make me laugh.

Kade was right on: I wouldn't really know unless I went. As my cheerleader, he made me give him my word I'd try.

Nine nineteen PM appeared on the clock. I was outside the room where the Betas were preparing the rush. I'd been there for twenty minutes. It was supposed to have started at nine on the dot. So much for that.

"No, they're not on CP Time," mumbled this dark girl with a midlength bob cut and a slamming body.

"I know that's right," I said, not knowing if she even wanted me to hear her thoughts.

Next to the girl with the bob, another cute brown-skinned girl, about five-six and sporting a fly short do, said, "Hi, I'm Torian Palmer. This is my roommate, Loni Bolds. I see everyone else huddled around in groups, so they probably know each other. I really want to be a Beta. What about you?" she said, extending her hand.

"I'm Malloy Murray, and if they don't start soon, I'm leaving," I said, clearly making it known that I did not need this.

Loni said, "Exactly, Malloy. I'm not waiting all night either."

Torian said, "Wait—Murray, like in the National President's last name. You're the girl everyone has been talking about? You're her daughter? I didn't see you last year, so I didn't know what you looked like."

I felt awkward. I didn't want fake friends. However, as we waited for the Betas, I kept chatting with the two girls. They seemed real cool. They were both business majors like me. We were all sophomores, and as we looked around, we noticed that most of the girls were juniors who hadn't made the line last year. Everyone looked nervous. And, like Torian, if the doors didn't open till next week, they weren't moving.

"These girls are like zombies," Loni uttered, completely taking the words from my brain as she discreetly pointed to the group nearby. "My old roommate and her crew, they're all juniors. You can see how desperate they are to make it."

"Why aren't you with them?" I asked.

"They've been doing underground stuff with the Betas for a month now, and they just know I ain't gonna make line now, because I refuse to let them whip my butt."

"Well, let's not say what we won't do," Torian said.

"Please, I think they're crazy to let someone hit 'em. No one is putting any marks on me," I told the two of them emphatically.

Hayden opened the doors thirty-five minutes late and

said, "Thanks for your patience. We had to wait on our adviser before we could begin."

Another Beta peered from behind her and said, "I'm Bea, the Vice President, and I see some girls want to be Betas bad. Come on in. Welcome to our rush."

At that moment I wanted to turn and walk away. I didn't want to get lumped with overzealous girls badly needing Greek letters to define them. I was a confident somebody. I might not be the nicest, but I was secure. However, Loni and Torian had sandwiched me between them. They wanted me going nowhere but into the room. Their warm smiles were comforting. Not backing out, I walked with them.

It turned out to be an enjoyable night, probably because a lot of ladies from the alumni chapter and Sharon were absent, for whatever reason. Though I had grown up with the organization plastered everywhere in my house, seeing my mother on a video as the National President talk about the joy of the sorority moved me. She described how the sisterhood brought out her love for others. And then when she went on to say how proud she was of their impact on the community and why she wanted us to think about being a Beta to do even more good for the world, that was even more impactful.

I couldn't say I was 100 percent ready to go for it, but I was certainly leaning that way. When the rush was over, Torian and Loni and I exchanged numbers. Maybe the whole pledge process wasn't going to be as bad as I thought. Yeah, I was starting to feel it.

*   *   *

"This is an excellent package. You're going to make line, I just know it," my mom said at the University of Southeastern Arkansas football game against a big rival. "You've got all the necessary items required in here. And your application is really stellar."

We were supposed to be watching my brother play, but she had her head plunged into my rush packet. I was sort of mad at her for not enjoying the moment. I wanted to watch the game like all the other spectators. She kept interrupting me every five minutes about why I wrote this or that. Then it dawned on me, as I watched my dad in the row in front of us laugh and be all into this lady ten years younger than him, that my mom needed a distraction. I wouldn't say my mom still loved my dad, but I knew somewhere deep inside she still had some feelings for him. I had been in high school when they broke up. I still didn't know the details of why they split.

I did remember my mom saying her life had been like one of the characters from the movie, *Waiting to Exhale*. She felt she'd helped my dad soar and become a successful executive. And as soon as it happened, her version was that he dumped her for a white lady. Except, my dad never tried to marry the lady, he just moved out with my brother and was able to dip out and have fun whenever he wanted without my mom nagging him. But now that he had gotten the blondes out of his system, it seemed he was into this young girl. For the first time in a long time I understood why my mom clinged so heavily to the sorority. She was able to receive from her sisters the fulfillment, joy, passion, and love she looked for and expected in a marriage. Plus, she was retired, and the organization gave her much to do.

"You think it's good, Mom?" I said, rubbing her back as I felt her pain.

She smiled. "This is excellent!"

Arkansas was up 14–0, when the defense came out. I started cheering.

"Somebody is really excited, and your brother is on the sidelines. This boy, Kade, from the convention has your attention, huh? Just don't get too caught up," she said, obviously telling from the expression on my face that I had a big thing for Kade.

She cared about my feelings, and she didn't want me to get hurt. Though I knew this was always how she felt about me, it was nice to hear her say it.

Later in the game, I was texting Loni and Torian back and forth, trying to convince them to come up to Arkansas for the party. My mom was pleased that I was trying to pledge her sorority and making friends who were trying to do the same, so she told me to invite them to the national headquarters office soon. I wasn't sure I'd do that, but she was so insistent, I told her I'd ask them.

Life wasn't bad. After being in school for six weeks, I still had all As. Regardless of what happened with the Betas, I was developing friendships. And my man was on the attack, sacking the quarterback play after play, coming off the defensive end.

Then, on the next play, when Kade took somebody down, Kade didn't get up. Most of the game, I had been playing it cool, keeping my excitement for my guy under wraps from fans. But at that moment, I screamed.

I didn't even know my dad had known we were dating, but he turned around and said, "It's Kade, huh?"

"I need to go down to the field."

"We can go to the locker room. I've got a parent pass," he said as I stood and walked with him to the tunnel.

"Dad, I didn't know you knew we were dating?"

"Yeah, I hang out with Mikey and Kade all the time. Lately the boy has been just extra clingy and overly nice to me. Then he started talking about my daughter. I wondered what was going on with you two, and Mikey confirmed it. Next time I saw that joker, I told Kade I'd kill him if he didn't do right by you. He assured me he had the best intentions. The boy really does care. He's trying to get an internship this summer if this football thing doesn't work out. He really does have potential."

I just hugged my father and whispered, "Now stop messing with my babysitters."

"Staying young, that's all. No harm done."

In the locker room, he went over to the side and said a few things to the trainer. The next thing I knew, we were ushered to stand next to a lady. My dad knew her.

"Oh, Mr. Murray, thank you for coming down to see Kade. Goodness gracious, my son, my son. I don't know what I'm gonna do."

It was his mom. My heart was tearing, but hers was clearly broken. She threw her large hands up in the air and started talking about everything in the world so she wouldn't concentrate on what was bothering her most.

"Who in the world does this little girl think she is coming back here to check up on her investment? I am sick of these hot-tailed girls wanting to see my son play at any cost," she said to my dad as she turned her nose up at me.

Maybe I'd be territorial, too, if my boy was projected to make a ton of dough. Instinct kicked in, and I stepped back. I didn't want to disturb her.

My dad looked back and saw she was talking about me. "Uh, no, this is my daughter."

Like a microwave gets hot in seconds, she quickly warmed up to me. "Wow, you're Mikey's sister?"

I didn't get to respond. Kade was abruptly rolled inside, and his mom rightfully left me and my dad to go over to him. "You are not going back out there. I don't care what you say. This is crazy," she said to Kade.

I was so nervous, not knowing what was up. A few minutes later one of the trainers came to me and asked me to follow them to see Kade. I hadn't been a daddy's girl in a while. Now I was clinging to his arm.

"Dad, he's with his mom. I'm just down to make sure he's going to be all right. I don't want to intrude."

The trainer heard me and said, "No, it's okay, he wants to see you."

My dad pushed me toward the guy. A part of me didn't want to see Kade hurt at all. I needed to be strong for him. I couldn't be vulnerable.

"Hey, baby," Kade said as he extended his hand. "No long face. They say it's just sprained and that I can go back out there. I see you met my mom."

"I just thought you were Mikey's sister and came down with your dad," his mom said in a mean tone. "Is there something else going on I don't know about? Maybe I didn't have her pegged wrong after all."

"Ma, leave her alone, she's my girl."

"What? You telling me someone is your girl?" She turned to me. "Okay, then, talk some sense into this fool and tell him not to go back out there on that field."

He made the argument. "NFL pro scouts are here."

"So?" I said to him.

"Malloy, they came to see me play, and I'm trying to keep my stock up so I can go in the first round."

"You've already had two fumbles, and three sacks. If you didn't impress them today, I need to take their job. You don't need to go back in the game. Let your leg get stronger, and next week you can go back out there. If you go out now you might damage it and be out a few more games. You don't want that now, do you? Come on now."

"All right!" he huffed. "Wrap me up. I'm just going to sit on the sidelines. I'll see you after the game."

The trainer wheeled him back into the isolated part of the locker room. I walked out to my dad. His mom followed me.

"You really care for my son, and you've got influence over him. Take care of him. He's a hothead, but if he can appreciate someone with your qualities, maybe my boy is growing up. All right, Big Mike, take care, now."

"You impressed the mom. Dang!" my dad teased. "I taught you well."

"Keep being a good influence and lose the young girl," I said as I hit him in the arm.

"Stay out of your daddy's business," he joked. "Ain't nothing that serious. Just messing with your mama."

* * *

"Okay, so maybe you coming to this party is not a great idea," I said as I saw my boyfriend hopping toward me at the big afterparty the team was throwing later that night.

"Please, we beat them Eagles real bad! Your brother got an interception. I've got to be here for him anyway, and then maybe you and I can have some alone time. I don't have a curfew, but I have to be with the trainer early in the morning."

Worried, I said, "You don't need to be on your feet that long."

"Come here, girl," he said as he threw his arm around me and drew me to him.

If eyes could cut, I would have had so many stabs up and down my back. Most of the women in the place were checking us out, and, yes, when I first met Kade, I, too, had been physically attracted him. But getting to know him like I had over the last month—he was so deep. His kind of commitment would scare most of these women away. I knew why Sharon wasn't trying to give up that kind of affection.

Being naughty, Kade whispered, "You know I ain't had none in a month?"

"Well, we've been talking for thirty-two days. Is there something you need to be telling me?"

"You know I can't count good. My head is still messed up from the game."

"You play defense. You hit people. Nobody hits you."

"Come on, I'm on crutches. Somebody hit me."

I lightly jabbed him. "All right. Quick on your feet, too!"

"Let's go sit down," he said as he grabbed my waist.

"There's nowhere to sit."

"I'm going to go find us some chairs. You just stay right here."

Before I could tell him I'd go, I was distracted. My phone started buzzing. I looked down and saw I had a text message from Loni that said she and Torian were at the door. My brother was working the door, so I asked, "Can they get in free, please?"

"They your friends? You ain't got no friends," Mikey joked as I popped him. "If y'all can put up with my mean sister, come on in. I'm Mikey."

I bragged, "He's the guy who got the interception today, y'all."

"So you find time to notice my game, too."

"Oh, see, you got jokes." I turned to Torian and Loni. "Come on, girls. I want you to meet my boo." Then I turned and saw Sharon was rubbing all over Kade's chest. "Oh, no! This hussy is not up in here trying to get with my man."

"Okay, so who's your man?" Loni asked.

"Yeah, which one is he?" Torian repeated.

I pointed to Kade. Torian and Loni saw all the Betas around him. They tugged me back from walking over.

Torian said, "You can't date one of the Beta guys. That's pledging suicide. Uh-uh!"

The music got lower, and Kade and Sharon's voices escalated. He was stepping back from her. She was ticked. I didn't feel threatened. I knew he didn't want her.

"Clearly what they had is over," I said boldly to my friends.

"Sharon, move back now. I said we're over. I'm not trying to be mean. Plus, I'm hurt. I can't have you tugging on me."

"But I need to talk to you Kade; this is serious."

"Ain't nothing left to say."

He looked over and saw me watching. I couldn't believe it when he hobbled over, bent his neck down, and planted his lips on mine. People in the room started clapping and cheering. Sharon and a few of the Betas from Western Smith fled the party.

"Stop, stop, you can't do this," I said

"I just want you to know, Malloy, that Sharon and I are over for real. I don't want nobody making you feel like that ain't clear." He started moaning, and I knew his ankle was hurting him.

"Let me go get my car so I can take you home."

In a sexy voice he said, "Oh, I like the sound of that."

"Guys, I've got to leave," I said to Torian and Loni.

Loni looked around and saw the crowd getting loud again. "We're going to leave, too."

"Y'all don't like the party?"

"No, it's just that we got some crazy looks from the Betas, and we aren't even supposed to be out like this," Loni said. "You know, when you want to pledge, sisters don't want you out."

"Y'all gonna let them dictate your life? You've got to have some fun."

"No, we'll go," Torian said as they walked out with me.

When we got to my car, I yelled. "Oh, my gosh!"

My back window had been smashed in. There was a brick with a note stuck to it written in brown lipstick that read

Don't be such a slut! I was livid. "That chick is crazy!" I yelled. "I cannot believe this!"

"Calm down!" Torian said. "You don't know who did this."

"Are you kidding me? I know exactly who did this. It was Sharon."

PRINCIPLE

I just stared at the note as tears of anger streamed down my face. The party that was once inside was, I guess, now over because everyone had piled around me. I heard some folks laughing, and when I looked up it was the Betas from my school.

"Who would do this?" someone screamed out from behind me.

"Did you leave a purse or anything out?" Loni said.

"I know who did this. I think it's mighty trifling that the trick can't come up in my face and handle this woman to woman!" I yelled out as I looked across the parking lot straight into the eyes of Sharon. "I'm going right over there to talk to her."

"Oh, no, you are not. You're not going anywhere," Torian said, holding me back. "Loni, help me."

Loni chimed in. "Yeah, she's right. You'll be committing suicide if you go over there."

"Listen to you guys. What kind of frame of mind are you in? Will you do anything to pledge and get stupid Greek letters?" I was so angry, looking at the shattered glass. "A brick was just thrown through my car window by one of them girls because now her guy is with me. I tried to let him go. I tried to give him back to her. It's not my fault he didn't want her. If this is the dumb stuff she does, no wonder Kade wanted to end it. She's older than me and still acting like a child."

I kicked my foot in the air. I banged on my car window. People must have thought I was out of my mind as well. But seeing this foolishness, I couldn't hold it together.

"I don't even want to think about pledging. I'm calling my mom right now." I reached in my pocket to get my cell.

After I had explained everything to my mother, I got the third degree. "Malloy, what are you doing out this late at a party anyway?"

"Mom, I know you're in bed, and I'm sorry. I just came to the party with Mikey. Now I can't go home because one of your Betas threw a brick through my window."

More sympathetic, she asked, "You weren't in the car, were you, baby?"

"No, Mom, the car was parked. I came out here and found it like that."

"So, wait a minute . . . back up, Malloy. How do you know one of the Betas did it? It's that cocky, popular guy you're dating, huh? You took somebody's boyfriend."

"Mom, how can I take somebody's boyfriend?"

"Malloy, don't be silly. You know men say anything. I recall when that young man came up to the Beta convention with Mikey to see his girlfriend. Now, I told you earlier today . . ."

I wasn't even listening as she went on and on. Everything around me was such a blur. Torian and Loni were trying to tell me Sharon didn't do this, but who else would have a motive to mess up my ride, freak me out, and leave me a crazy note trying to scare me away from Kade? It could be only Sharon. Was I the only sane one living in a crazy world?

"Mom, I gotta go. I'm about to call the police."

"Malloy Murray, I'm telling you don't do that. Let's not make it a big deal. I'll pay for the window tomorrow. Tell your brother to let you drive his car. You call me as soon as you get back to your apartment."

"Mom, I don't even see Mikey anywhere around here. I have money in my bank account to pay for the window. That's not even the point. The one who did this should pay for it, and I know who did it. Precious sorority sister or not, she is going to pay."

My mom yelled back, "Now, you listen here! You didn't see anybody do anything. Calm your little self down. You shouldn't have been out there this late anyway. I told you nothing good happens out late at night in them streets. Some lessons you just have to learn the hard way, and obviously this is one of them. Malloy, am I making myself clear? You hear what I am saying to you? This is over. No police. We will take care of it on our own."

"Mom, I don't want to pledge, okay?"

"And quit saying all that, too. You're all hot under the

collar. As soon as any little thing happens, you don't want to pledge. That's why you need to be in a sorority. So you can get some discipline and understand what sisterhood is all about."

"If sisterhood is someone coming over to my car and breaking it because they can't have their little way, I don't want to be a part of the sisterhood! It seems like a whole bunch of sisters from the hood, if you ask me," I blurted as I hung up.

I wanted to smash my phone through the window that was still in one piece—vandalize my own car, that's just how frustrated I was from hearing my mom side with her stupid sorors. I knew we didn't have the best mother-daughter relationship, but I certainly wished she would have taken my side for once. I had thought we were gaining ground. Why she kept standing up for those girls who wore lavender and turquoise was beyond me. When would her own daughter come first? As I listened to Loni and Torian tell the crowd to mind their own business and I looked at the crushed glass all over my backseat, deep in my heart I knew I would never get all my mom's love unless I was a Beta.

"Come on, now, we just asked y'all to leave. You see she's upset about her car, dang!" Torian yelled out.

Though I was disappointed that my new buddies didn't support my view that Sharon did this, I really appreciated the two of them having my back. Even if folks weren't listening, they didn't want me to be a sideshow. As I cried, they shielded my body from direct view.

After I got myself together, I finally looked up and saw only Torian. "Where's Loni? I'm sure she wanted to get away from this whole scene. I can't blame her—you can go, too. I'll be fine."

"No, no, she went inside to find your brother."

Dang, I thought, *they really are good friends*. I did need to find Mikey. Why he wasn't out here, I didn't know. When we were growing up, he could always sense my tears as they formed and always came to my aid without me calling him. Not this time. In despair, I leaned over my vehicle.

"Dang, what y'all looking at?" I heard Kade yell.

When Kade came over to me, I rushed into his arms, and he held me tight. A part of me felt like all this was just a bad dream, but now, in his embrace, I was in a sweet slumber, and everything would be all right.

"What happened? Did you see who did this?"

"I know who did this!" I told him, feeling like the judge and jury.

The crowd wasn't going anywhere, because we were playing out a soap opera, and I really got folks talking when I popped my trunk and pulled out a crowbar. I wanted to bash Sharon's head in. I've never been a violent person. I don't fight, except for kicking Mikey's butt over the years. But Sharon had crossed the line when she'd vandalized my property. If my mom wasn't going to make her pay for it voluntarily, maybe a little blood would do me just fine.

"Where you going with that?" Kade asked as he grabbed the crowbar from my tight grasp.

"Give that back to me! I need to take care of business. It's on now!"

"You are not going to hit nobody. Did you see Sharon do this?"

"What, you taking her side, too?" I said, getting all

upset and defensive. "You're just like my mom and my girls telling me I'm not sure. Dude, you should have stayed with Sharon."

"Listen, calm down," he said as he pulled me close. "Baby, I want to be with you. Just because I don't want you to fight her doesn't mean I want to be with her. Come on, now, think logically on this one."

"Think logically. I'm trying to think logically. She's going to admit she did this. I'm going to scare a confession out of her bony behind right now. You can get on my side and join me, or you can get the heck out of my way." Because I was so angry, I shoved him to the side.

"Kade done met his match with that one!" someone in the crowd hollered.

"Kade, seems like you need to go back to the Beta!" somebody else shouted.

Then a group of Betas was walking toward us. I was happy—Sharon was coming my way. All I needed was the weapon.

"Somebody said you sayin' I did this. Don't be putting lies like that all out there," Sharon said as she got up in my face.

"Oh, so you think I'm scared of you?" I said, pushing her back.

Some of her sorority sisters grabbed her, and Kade grabbed me.

"Wait, wait, y'all, let me go. Let me go," Sharon said to them before she turned to Kade. She was smiling at him. My man, with his strength, put me behind him. He started listening to her. I was breathing so hard I was about to pop.

Sharon begged, "I need you, Kade. You don't under-stand what's going on with us. We have a deep connec-tion. I just need to help you see it. I need your time. You got to talk to me."

Kade would not let me get around him. "We were just inside, Sharon, going through this. Come on. Please don't make this end ugly. I'm with Malloy now."

"Malloy, Malloy—what can she give you that I can't? You feel like you've used me all up, and now you want fresh meat? Well, I got a news flash for you. She's no vir-gin."

I couldn't believe he still kept holding me back from beating down this chick. She had crossed the line in so many ways already. Now she was all up in my personal affairs even more.

Edging around Kade I said, "You don't know me, and you broke the wrong car window. You better be scared."

"Are you threatening me, Malloy?" Sharon asked.

"Please, Kade, let me talk to her," Hayden said as she moved Sharon back. "Please let me talk to Malloy." She added, "I can calm her down."

Because Hayden and I were working on our differences, I had no problem hearing her out. We walked over to the side. But Hayden just started talking trash. Like I owed Sharon a break. Hayden thought I was just gonna drop all this. Here I had thought she was going to apologize for her girl.

"Are you kidding me? She broke my car window. And I am just supposed to drop it? She's basically saying I'm some skank. Yet here you stand telling me I'm just sup-posed to move on from that? And then she has the nerve to accuse me of spreading lies about her? Whatever, Hayden, please get out of my way."

"You want to pledge. I'm trying to make that happen, but you're not making it easy. Who in my chapter is going to vote for you? She was with us, Malloy. Sharon did not break your window."

"Oh, so she was with you all night?" I asked, knowing it wasn't the truth.

"I mean, not all night, but she just went to the bathroom," Hayden said as I shook my head, knowing as close as the parking lot was, Sharon needed only a little time to destroy my car.

"It doesn't take long to grab a brick and throw it through my window. I watch *CSI*. I'm going to take my car to the police station and get her prints. That way, when they come after her tail with a warrant, you, Kade, and my mom will all stop being on her side. She broke my window, and that's a fact."

I still wanted to hit Sharon—until I got away from Hayden and I heard the last part of her conversation with Kade. She kept pleading for another chance. I've never seen a girl lose it so bad and be so desperate to try to hold on to a man. The two-hundred-fifty-dollar deductible I'd have to pay to get my window fixed paled in comparison to all the broken emotions I saw Sharon reveal.

"All right, so you gonna drop this now?" Kade said to me as he and I walked back into the building. "You see she can't take no more."

"All right, fine. Where's Mikey? I need to get his car and go home."

"I haven't seen your brother. Your friend was looking for him, and that's when she told me where you were. Mike's gone."

"We can take you home," Torian cut in, Loni by her side.

"I would take you home, baby, but I got to see the trainer at five in the morning for rehab. Gimme your key, and I'll drive your car over to Mike's place." Kade gave me a puppy-dog face, and I knew I needed to go with my friends and just call it a night.

"Come on, Malloy, let's get out of here," Loni said as she rubbed my back. "I know you're tired."

"Call me tonight, baby. It'll be all right," Kade said before he hobbled over to my car.

When I got in the backseat of Loni's car, I laid my head down. It was pounding something fierce. All I had been trying to do was enjoy my time with my guy at a party, and that couldn't even go well.

"Girl, I know how you feel," Loni said, surprising me. "If it would have been me, I probably would have wanted to whoop up on her, too."

"We just couldn't let you go down like that," Torian chimed in.

"It's obvious Kade likes you, though," Loni said as she kept her eyes on the road.

"Yeah, he really does," Torian said. "And he's a hottie!"

"What are y'all talking about?"

"The way he broke up with Sharon for, like, the fourth time in front of all them people? He tried to be nice to her, but she just wouldn't let up, being all clingy on him, grabbing on his shirt, trying to kiss him."

"She was doing all that?" I asked.

"Yeah, while you were talking to Hayden, she was show-ing that maybe she was loony enough to mess up your ride. She whispered some other stuff to him we couldn't hear. It appeared she was trying to tell him anything she could to hold on to him. But the fine brother wasn't buying it. He was completely into you," Torian said, turning in the front seat to give me the scoop.

"What did you do to hook him like that, girl?" Loni teased.

"I don't know. I just wasn't letting him play me. Trust me, though, if I knew he was going to be this much trou-ble—people breaking my car window and stuff—I never would have gotten back with his behind."

The two of them looked at each other and laughed. I was serious, though. Why women couldn't just walk away gracefully when a man was through with them was beyond anything I could conceive.

"Yeah, you would have gotten with him," Loni said.

"Yeah, you would have," Torian agreed.

"Okay, maybe I would have." I laughed as I thought about Kade.

We stopped at a nearby Waffle House—the only place open at three in the morning—and got a bite to eat. Torian and Loni thought my headache would go away if I put a little something in my stomach.

Once we were settled in our booth, Torian asked, "So, Malloy, you were saying Loni and I would do anything to pledge. You don't feel that way?"

"No, I don't feel that way. Now I really don't know if

I'm going to go through with that at all. If a person must lose their own identity to become a slave to somebody else—and allow reason to just go out the window—no, I don't want a part of that. I'm too strong-willed. Somebody will get killed in the process."

"Yeah, and I got a feeling it wouldn't be you," Torian said.

"Exactly," I replied, knowing I would never put up with foolishness. "Hazing, hitting me, and mentally abusing me—they can have it. They've been known to do it tons of times to past lines, and I know they have intentions to do it to us."

"I wish I could have some of your stamina," Loni said.

"Girl, you are not no pushover yourself. I saw you turning down them guys in there dancing tonight."

"Yeah, coming at me with bad breath, falling all over themselves all drunk and stuff, and one guy had a joint in his hand. Well, what do they think I am?"

"Weak, like most of the women at a party trying to get with anybody. Torian, you're strong, too."

"What are you talking about?"

"Taking on that whole crowd, telling them to get back. "

"It wasn't like they listened."

"Yeah, but it's not like you backed down and stopped trying to get them off my butt."

"What you expect us to do, girl? We care about you. What went down was unfortunate. Money is too hard to come by nowadays. Who has it to waste on replacing a window? I just hope it wasn't Sharon," Torian said.

The two of them talked so sincerely about how they cared about me, and knowing they were also women of strength, maybe we could all be true buddies. Unfortunately I didn't know what having good girlfriends felt like. Someone other than a relative who just wanted to try to make it better . . . that was somebody I wanted to be down with. Someone that would have your back on principle. That was a real bond.

BLEAK

It's funny how a week can make things so much better. I now had my car back and fixed. I was becoming quite close with Torian and Loni. I could really hang out with them. Fashion was my thing, so I noticed they both had unique styles. They didn't just wear store-put-together outfits. That was a sign we could be cool.

Kade and I had it going on as well. Though I hadn't seen him since the night of the party, we'd talked multiple times every day. My classes were still a breeze. Sirena had been really helpful to me as well, fixing the best dinners and snacks that helped me while I studied. Yeah, my life was good.

If I only could have gotten my mom off my back about the whole pledging thing, I would have been great. Packets were due the next day, and I hadn't even looked over mine since I'd seen my mom. I was going to see my mom at the national-organization headquarters right outside Little Rock because my godmom, the First Vice President, was in town. And my mom kept bugging me to bring my new buddies by to see Beta Gamma Pi's official space.

"Oh, wow, this place is more gorgeous than on the Web site," Torian said as she stepped into the entrance when we arrived.

There was a marble hallway that stretched out many feet in front of us. Hanging from the thirty-foot ceiling was a lovely crystal chandelier. The soft, dim lighting provided a relaxing ambience. It was quite a breathtaking place. I'd been here countless times before, but I'd never stopped to appreciate the view. But I didn't feel like I wanted today to be any different. Being stubborn I said, "It's all right."

"Come on, now, Malloy, 'its all right'?" Loni teased. "This place is special. All these pictures on the wall of past and present leaders makes me feel like I can fly to my dreams and do anything."

We walked past the turquoise-colored carpet in the founder's room. I couldn't get Torian and Loni to move past the door. They seemed to breathe it all in as if it were air. Finally they moved, and we headed to the room with the purple carpet. It was the National President's office.

"Oh, my gosh! I can't," Torian said, stopping just shy of us going in.

"Girl, please. Mom, were here!" I called out—like I had absolutely no home training or etiquette. I shoved Torian into the room. Loni hit me on the shoulder. They were really way too into this.

Loni leaned over and whispered, "You know you're wrong for doing that. This is a big deal to us."

"Yeah, to you," I said. I felt like someone was forcing me into something. "Girl, I do not want to be here."

"It's so crazy. So many girls across the country, trying to pledge Beta Gamma Pi right now, would kill to have their mom as the National President, and here you are. This is your real life, and you have no appreciation for it. Absolutely crazy to me," Torian said melodramatically.

"If you been where I been," I replied, "and had to put up with taking a backseat to this stuff all your life, you wouldn't be all nostalgic either, trust me."

"Young ladies, hello and welcome." My mom came out, hugging Torian and Loni.

She'd never met them a day in her life, but she was such the politician. She didn't, however, reach out her arms to me, probably a little unsure of how I was going to respond, as I'd already cut up a little bit during our entrance. But I couldn't play, act, or brush off the fact that I was ecstatic to see my godmom over in the corner. A dark-skinned lady, she was short in stature, but she was sassy. She didn't live in California—California lived in her. She was regal, upbeat, optimistic, lively, and charming, and everything about her said "I am an empowered black woman. Now what?"

After complete introductions were made, my godmother, Dr. Day, said, "So, ladies, Malloy's mom tells me you guys are trying to be Betas?"

"Yes, ma'am, we are," Torian said in a perky tone when she saw I wasn't going to answer.

I looked around the room and started whistling. My godmother wanted me to pledge just as badly as my mom. They both were going to be disappointed.

"Oh, come on, now, dear, I know you're not going to let us down."

I still couldn't respond. I didn't want to let her down. But I wasn't sure I could give her what she wanted either.

Dr. Day said, "You two stay here and speak to the National President. I'm going to take this lady here for a stroll."

As soon as we stepped out of my mom's office, I felt less pressure. My mom's eyes on me was always intense. I always felt like I was gonna let her down just by not standing correctly.

My godmother said, "Girl, I have prayed for you so much over the years."

"Yeah, and you've been there a lot for me, too, when my mama wasn't." I had to give her props.

"Okay, might be some truth in that. But are you aware of all the good things your mom has done for the world and in the community through her services to and through our organization?" I shook my head. "Well, Malloy, she's the president now, and this is a paid position for her. Yeah, unlike all the other sororities out there, we've recognized that just as the executive director gets paid, the National Presidency is a full-time job and should be paid as well." She waved for me to follow her.

"Where are we going?"

She unlocked the steel door. "This is our private room."

"This isn't reserved for Betas only, is it?" I asked as we went into a dark space.

"No, it's . . . it's not." She flipped on the switch, and on the wall were thank-you letters from different mayors, counselmen, lawyers, and everyday people.

Squinting my eyes, I asked, "What am I supposed to make of all this?"

"Don't just read the headlines. You have got to read deeper, my dear." My godmother saw me still not getting it and took me by the hand. "When the white racist talk-show host got on the radio and degraded the first black homecoming queen of a predominately white school, your mom petitioned for his resignation and won. She made that man understand the depth of hurt and pain he caused many generations of young women. One discrimination case after another, your mom has been a social activist making change for our country. Here, a wrongfully convicted man was about to get out of the death penalty. Do you see this?"

"Yeah," I said. A tear almost came to my eye as I looked at the picture of the badly beaten man.

"Because your mom got behind him, this young man is free. A lot of these people had no hope before Beta Gamma Pi got into the mix and exposed their unfortunate situation. I know there's a lot still wrong with our organization, but we need strong ladies like you to continue to make change. Beta Gamma Pi might have taken a piece of your childhood, but it can add so much more to your future if you let it. Join your mom and me in this great cause. Beta Gamma Pi needs you."

I wanted so badly to ignore everything she was saying, but it stuck to my heart. What was I going to do?

A week later, I couldn't believe I was at the Beta Gamma Pi interview. Why was I doing this? Well, I'd convinced myself that all the good the organization stood for far outweighed all the reasons I wanted to stay away. Though I felt my mom had cheated me, she loved me with all her heart. This was her way of being the best mom she could be. I had to give this a try.

Surprisingly the first part of my interview went very well in front of the Betas and the adviser. I truly thought the Betas hated me, but they were overly cordial and all business. Obviously I had misjudged the group.

"Great, thank you. That'll be all," Hayden said to me.

When I was ushered out, the chapter adviser followed me. "Now, you tell that mom of yours we took real good care of you."

"Yes, ma'am," I said. I saw four other girls waiting to go in. "You guys aren't done, are you?"

"We're taking a break for fifteen minutes. These young ladies are early. Got to go pick up my kids from school and run them home right around the corner. I'll be right back before they start up, or they'll have to wait. But, honey, you did so great."

That was fine and dandy and all, but I wanted to make it on my own merit. No special treatment needed. Fair and just was all I asked for, and I knew deep down that would be all my mom would want.

As I went to look for my keys, I realized my purse wasn't on me.

A door opened, and the Vice President, Bea, yelled out, "Malloy, I think you left your purse!"

Darn it, she was right. I walked back to the room to get it. Bea didn't hand it to me, though. She actually tugged me back inside the door and slammed it.

"Round two of the interview. Okay, let's get down to

business for real!" Sharon shouted out. "Sit, trick! Why do you think we'd ever want someone as disgusting as you to be a part of our group?"

"Disgusting?" I said, trying to maintain my composure. "I don't go around bashing in people's windows. Besides, when men tell me they don't want to be with me anymore, I let them go. I don't get mad at another female when I can't hold on to my man, and if I was a part of any kind of sorority trying to do good for the community, I would always seek out women with my characteristics."

I looked hard into Sharon's face and rolled my eyes. I could not believe I had been thinking they were cool after all. These girls were now holding me here without an adviser present. Though I knew I could jet, I was ready for their heat.

"Okay, see, that's just it right now—she's accusing me of breaking her window," Sharon said as she took off her earrings and came charging toward me.

"I thought this was an interview. If you guys wanted to ask me some serious questions, I could sit here another few minutes without your adviser, even though I know this little one-sided chat is illegal."

"What, are you threatening us?" some tall girl hollered from the back.

A Beta who wore a pin with the name Dena on it pointed at me. "I haven't even seen you at any of our events. What events have you come to?"

"I'm taking a heavy course load this semester—"

She quickly cut me off. "And what about last semester?"

"I actually did attend a Beta Gamma Pi event for another school this summer."

Sharon yelled, "Oh, but you're trying to pledge Alpha chapter here, and you haven't been to our functions! Plus, going to parties don't count. You think we should let you on?"

"Again, I didn't think you were letting me on because I've come to your stuff. I thought you were letting me on because I could add to what you may do in the future."

"Are you getting smart with me?" Sharon asked.

"Listen, ladies, I want to be a part of what you're doing, I do." I couldn't believe I was uttering those words.

All of them looked like a bunch of barracudas waiting to eat me alive. I was trying to see past their yuckiness. But if it didn't work out, I wouldn't be crushed.

"Okay, that's more like it," the president said.

"Don't be thanking her," Sharon said to Hayden.

The door opened up, and the adviser came in. She looked at me strangely. I knew she wondered why I was back in there. I grabbed my purse and smiled at her. The Betas frowned at my exit. I knew my odds would be against me making their line. Whatever!

"Hey, y'all, what's up?" I said as I opened my door the next day to Loni and Torian. "Okay, neither one of you guys are smiling. What's going on? Y'all look all right, so I know nobody is hurt. What's up?"

"Why are you looking at us?" Torian said to Sirena, alerting me to the fact that Sirena was listening in the hallway.

"She's cool," I said to my friends as I stuck my head out my door and waved. "Hey, girl."

"Hey, I just was making sure you knew them."

"Yeah, these are—"

Sirena squinted her face. "Who, who are they?"

"Why she got to tell you? Come on," Torian said as she pulled Loni in and slammed the door.

"Now, you know that was rude," I said.

Torian said, "Come on, Malloy, the girl was all up in your business. We got more serious stuff to handle than some girl that don't have a life."

"Girl, that used to be me. I didn't have friends and all this other stuff till you guys came in the picture, trying to make me pledge and all that."

Torian got excited. "What? Tell me. You got your letter? A call?"

"No, and don't you two try to save my feelings. It was no big deal that I didn't get invited in. You don't have to put on a face. This is October, not April Fool's. You can be excited if you got in."

But they weren't smiling. They weren't opening up. They weren't overjoyed, and they showed me no official letters.

Loni sank down in my bed and said, "You know what? I just really wanted this. I'm trying to stay positive about it, but it's just so unfair. All these girls are getting letters that have like a 2-something GPA; mine is 3.5. Yours is what, Torian?"

Torian said, "Mine is 3.0."

Loni continued venting. "And you said you didn't get a letter. Malloy, you had what, a 3.9?"

I nodded.

"And who wrote your letter?" Loni asked.

"My godmother."

Loni rationalized, "So the First National Vice President wrote your letter, and you didn't make line."

"How do you guys know we didn't for real?"

"Everybody has gotten their letters. Word is if you didn't get anything this morning, you'll be getting the no-thanks letter next week," Loni said.

Torian looked away. "I think it's because we've been hanging out with you."

Trying to be real about it, I said, "Guys, we've just been hanging out for, what, a couple weeks?"

"Yeah, but that's the most crucial time," Torian said in a salty tone. "Ever since we've been together, they've been having little events here and there, and we haven't been going."

I detested the fact that many girls trying to pledge a sorority felt that participating in illegal pledge activities was all right. Anything outside of the programs that were sanctioned by the national organization was underground activity. This was forbidden for a reason. Yet lots of people felt true pledging could be handled only with off-the-record stuff. If the only way to become a legit Beta was to have someone demean you with violence, they could count me out.

"I never stopped you," I said. "You want to get your head bashed in, then more power to you."

"I knew I should have pledged Rho Tau Nu," Torian said. "Friendlier than the girls here."

"Oh, you think so?" Loni said.

"Maybe, and why wouldn't they want me? My Beta interview went well."

"My first one did, too," I said, "but then I had another one that was crazy."

Torian said, "Yeah, we tried to call you afterward when we hadn't heard from you. We didn't know if you were participating in some of that underground stuff because you hadn't returned our calls and had left us out."

"I'm sorry about that, y'all. I'm just not used to having to check in with girlfriends. I've gone to none of their sets."

"It's cool. Your mom is going to be so hurt, too," Torian said.

"I tried. I mean, why is she going to be disappointed? It's not that I didn't go after it. They just decided not to put me on."

Torian said, "Yeah, I don't think she's going to be mad at you, but she'll be sad that all the hopes and dreams she has for you weren't realized. The things she wants you to gain out of this whole pledge experience will never be."

Loni added, "She was really pumped that we were hanging out."

Torian said, "She says you've always been a loner."

"Yeah, because I had friends in middle school who backstabbed me. That stuff hurt like something I'll never forget, and I just said I wasn't going to let a girl have that power anymore. Particularly a group of them."

"Funny, it has always been just the opposite for me," Torian said. "I've always stuck my neck out for my girlfriends. We've had issues, but deep down I knew how much I cared for them. I'd make sure that good was done in their life, and if I could change any of the pain they'd ever go through, I would. That's just what deep friendship and true sisterhood is all about."

I thought about what the two of them said, and I tried to make our evening fun. I cooked some steaks on my George Foreman Grill, and I even pulled out some girlie movies, putting my homework aside. But Torian and Loni weren't getting happier. They kept checking their e-mail to see if they'd gotten an electronic letter.

I knew Torian was right. The reason they weren't going to make line was really because they had been hanging out with me, and because the girls in the chapter had a personal vendetta with me that had nothing to do with my friends. I so wanted to help my girls get their dream. I genuinely cared that they were hurting, and I didn't want their outlook to stay bleak.

GIGANTIC

"What do you mean, you didn't make line?"

"No, not me, Mom. I'm not calling about me," I said to my mother over the phone as her voice got extremely angry, hearing that her precious Betas had omitted my two qualified friends and myself from their line.

"Yes, I understand about your two friends. They were lovely ladies. I haven't read all their information, but I'm certain they would have been great candidates, particularly if you say so. But I know your package was more than tight, and the adviser told the Regional Coordinator you shined. They didn't put you on? Oh, no."

"Mom," I said as I got up and went into my bedroom and closed the door.

Torian and Loni had looked extremely excited when they'd seen me calling my mom on their behalf. The last thing I wanted to happen was for my mom to turn it all around and get only me on line, when I wasn't even sweating about not being chosen. She had to understand that.

After I talked it through, she said, "I hear what you're saying."

"Do you, Mom, because I don't want you to get me put on just because."

"Well, you need to understand that they can't just pick and choose who they want without true justification as to why you guys didn't make it. Somebody not liking you—that's an unacceptable reason. They can't even hold it against you that your mom is the National President. And you think if those jokers were smart enough they would have put you on just because. But, again, I know your stuff was pristine."

"So can I tell my friends we're on?"

"No, no. You can't tell anybody anything. The Regional Coordinator has to handle this. Let me call her and get her involved. Tell your friends not to worry and just to have faith. And I'm so glad you called me, Malloy, because if the ceremony had happened and I didn't protest it in time, there'd be nothing I could do. But right now I can't believe this, and there is a lot I can do."

Because my mom worked on a national level for Beta Gamma Pi, I knew too much about the organization. There was a Pi ceremony, the induction ceremony where girls took their first pledge into the illustrious group. Then there were five gem ceremonies that each provided a special piece of training and vow that moved a person closer toward intake. Lastly there was the big ceremony, where a person actually became initiated. But you could only be initiated if you went through all the ceremonies. It was an all-or-nothing pledge process. But if they didn't want me to be a part of their organization, forget them. Why couldn't my mom see that?

"And you really want me to be a part of this sorority?"

"Well, we all have drama. We all have problems, but that doesn't mean it can't get better. So let me take care of what I need to take care of, and I'll be in touch. Smooches."

"Bye, Ma."

"Tell us what she said," Torian said as she swung open my bedroom door and waited for my response.

"Well, I don't need to tell you—it looks like you were eavesdropping."

Torian smiled and came closer. "I could hear only your part of the conversation. I didn't hear what she said."

"Let's back up, Torian, and give her space," Loni said rationally.

"Yeah, we just gotta chill right now. I don't know nothing. But she is going to try."

I didn't know how to respond when Torian suddenly hugged me real tight. It was the first time I'd ever experienced that kind of gratefulness. Quickly I pulled back. A part of me still didn't want to get too close. I still wasn't used to this girlfriend stuff. And another part wanted to hug Torian back and tell her how I felt about her friendship. But for now I had to be real.

"Listen, I know my mom's got pull and everything, but she didn't say we'd make line for sure."

"I know, I know, but it's just the thought that you tried," Torian said as she reached over and hugged me again. "Oh, my gosh, Malloy, thank you."

* * *

The next morning, I awoke not to my alarm clock but to the pounding of my door. I had a gut feeling it was Sirena. I didn't want to be rude to her and tell her I wasn't up for breakfast or a morning chat, as she'd been begging me to do with her for the last week. I thought if I'd ignored her, she'd understand I was tired and leave me alone, but her pounding just kept getting louder and louder and more persistent. Finally I dragged myself out of bed and went to the door.

"Yes?" I said in an irritated tone as I wiped my eyes and saw someone other than whom I expected. Hayden was standing before me. She didn't even ask if she could come in. She just walked right past me.

Frowning, she said, "Okay, look, I'm just gonna keep it real. Your mom made her calls. She played the ace card. You and those other two that we didn't want are on line."

I looked back at her, unimpressed. I didn't know if she wanted me to get on my knees and bow down to her, so I just looked at her. I mean, she wasn't doing me any favors by coming over here and giving me the news in person. It was obvious they didn't like me, and I wasn't gonna go away quickly and quietly. There was no reason I didn't make line. I had probably been more qualified then any of them already in the chapter. As much as I tried to denounce it, I had Beta Gamma Pi royalty running through my blood. I knew more facts and history about the organization than I wanted to admit. As she stood there looking smug at me, I wasn't going to back down and make her think I thought she was superior. Heck to the naw! When she kept staring, I said, "So, anything else you've got to say?"

"I suggest you quit before you even get in, Malloy. It'll be a big mess if you don't."

I opened the front door. She handed me a packet of information, walked out, and before she could say another smart word, I slammed the door in her face.

"What are y'all looking at?" I said to the other seven girls who kept staring at Torian, Loni, and myself as we waited to be inducted as Pis in the first iniation ceremony.

We were in the historic theater building on campus. I hated being in the cramped actors' dressing room off to the side. The air was so thick with female judgment I could have sworn we were outside dealing with smog. Loni had a body to die for, and her outfit was very fitted. Torian was just too perky and confident for the girls staring at us, I guess. Girls were hating.

It was no secret the other seven girls had been prepledging. I wasn't trailing them or anything, but they were on line illegally because they'd been underground for a while. They even looked malnourished. They all looked like if I put a burger in front of them, they'd tear it up. The three of us looked fresh, but those girls looked like hags. No style, no fashion, and no flare. Yuck. Actually, no part of me wanted to be with them. I could not imagine us as sisters. If we were sisters, I'd take them in the back room and change their clothes. But we weren't, so I kept my thoughts to myself. And if they thought underground activities were making them beautiful, they needed a mirror. No sister would have me looking like crap.

Thankfully they had all made it through the application process. Last year the talk had been that most of the girls on the underground line hadn't even been selected to be on the real line. Why take such a gamble? You mentally tear me down and then you don't even lift me up to the line. Not!

"Girl, don't be so mean to them," Torian said to me as she yanked me to the side. "They're never gonna like us that way."

I looked at Loni. "You better school your girl."

"Yeah," Loni said. "Torian, because we got put on line, they're not gonna like us anyway."

There was still the big question: why I was doing this. I mean, I knew it was going to make my mother happy, and a part of me liked being places where people thought they could keep me out. However, looking around at the brutal stares, I could have been doing way more with my time than putting up with these girls. My cell phone rang.

"You're not supposed to have a phone!" one girl shouted. "They collected them weeks ago, but you weren't here."

I looked at the phone, saw it was Kade, and answered it. "Hey, baby. Hold on one second." I went over to the girls and said, "Listen, I know y'all got beef with us, and I really don't care. I wasn't here a few weeks ago, but I'm here now. I haven't pledged nobody's nothing yet. I can do what I want, when I want. Now stay out of my business. Hey babe," I said into the phone.

"Dang, girl! Who you talkin' to?" Kade asked.

"I'm about to do this whole crazy pledge thing. Talk me out of it now, please!"

"You about to pledge? I don't understand. Sharon told me you didn't get an invite. That's why I was calling you, thinking we could get together. I just assumed you'd be somewhere sulking or whatever."

"Okay, so you think it's gonna slide past me that you been talking to Sharon?" I said to him, not happy at all that she was glad to give my man my bad news.

"Let me clarify. I just read her text. Don't need to get in trouble over my own words. I've been at school and football wishing I could be with you so you can rub me down. I'm aching, baby."

Relieved, I said, "I miss you, too, sweetie. For some crazy reason I just feel like I gotta do this. My mom got me on, so the drama is on."

"You got it like that? I understand. I love the ladies in the lavender and turquoise. But I miss my boo and need her with me," he said.

"Aw, I wish I could be with you, too. I just don't know when that's gonna happen. This all is so crazy, and I'm already on the hot seat."

"Well, don't let none of them girls break you down. I love your spirit. You would not be you if you marched to the beat of a plain drum."

"Thanks." We said our good-byes and hung up.

"No, you don't need to go over there." The girl who had told me to get off the phone tried to hold back the shortest girl in the room. But the little bitty chick pranced over to the three of us anyway. "Okay, so I'm Tammie with an *I-E*."

Without a care, I said, "Okay. I'm Malloy."

"I'm Torian." My friend perked up and offered her hand.

"Loni," my laid-back buddy said, not as thrilled.

"Why are you over here?" I asked, getting right to the point.

"Everybody tells me you're mean as a snake and can read right through people, so I appreciate your candor. Hopefully you appreciate mine."

"I'm not mean, am I," I said, looking at Torian and Loni as the two of them just laughed.

"I know my line sisters are a little ticked that you guys didn't go through none of the stuff we went through. A little bit of brutality, a little bit of emotional distress—"

"You asked for that by showing up for underground stuff, right?" I cut in.

"No, no. I'm just saying that's why they're upset. But I'm not upset. I'm honored to have the National President's daughter on my line. So while a lot of people plan not to associate themselves with you, I can give you some inside information in return for a little bit of special privilege."

"What are you talking about?" I asked as she rambled.

"Word is your mama is here for this ceremony. I want to meet her." Tammie pointed to her crew. "All them will be there hoping she talks to them, but you can introduce me."

"She'll do it," Torian insisted.

Tammie leaned in and said, "Smart move. The inside information I'll bring to you three will eventually help win them over."

The ceremony was about to begin. I was at the back of the line, being the tallest. Loni and Torian were next to each other in the middle, which was great. I didn't care that no one talked to me, but the two of them would need each other to get through all the tension. As soon as we were ushered into the building, my mother was on the stage conducting the ceremony, as she was the highest-ranking Beta in the place. The passion glistening in her eye captured my heart. I never saw her smile brighter.

When we entered the dark room, I felt like I was in a church sanctuary. The candles were glowing all over—there had to be over one hundred. We were walking on a white silk aisle that had lily petals scattered throughout. It was a breath of fresh air.

"These strong black women are proud in their own right, ready to make a difference. I am humble that you stand ready to replace the *I* in your life—the self-centered part of you—with Pi, a piece of our grand sorority. That you may embrace the sisterhood no matter how difficult it may be. The love for your Pi sisters will always be real, will always be deep, will always be pure. Please take the washcloth, place it in the basin, and cleanse your face clean. May that be the symbol of the first big step you will take toward our sisterhood."

Together we recited, "We are stronger when our bond is genuine." Though I said the words, I had no idea if that would ring true in my heart.

After the ceremony, everyone in the place gathered around my mother. You would have thought she was famous or something. I mean, she wasn't the pope or the President of the United States, but they were certainly treating her like royalty. For goodness sake, she was just my mom, but I had to remember that to them she was their leader. She certainly was a true picture of grace and dignity. A part of me really appreciated all that she was as I watched her sincerely give every person time. This was more than just some job to her. This was her duty, her calling, her core.

"Okay, so you can introduce me anytime," this little annoying voice said from behind.

I didn't have to turn to see that it was Tammie with an *I-E.* I walked right over to my mom, and she acknowledged me right off. I didn't have to wait or anything. I actually felt special.

"Mom, this is Tammie."

"One of your line sisters, wonderful," my mom said as she gave the short, self-assured girl a quick hug. "Tammie, I know it's been a little bumpy having three more people added to the line, but embrace all the passengers, because the airplane is in the air now. I know you *all* will soar to greatness together."

I wasn't a dummy. My mom was trying to make sure my line sister knew she expected them to welcome me. She was a lioness protecting her cub, but I wanted to roar on my own. I tried to walk away and give them space, but my mom tugged at my hand.

"Yes, ma'am," Tammie said. "I just want to say that my mom is a Beta, and she said you're the best president in the sorority's history."

"Oh, wow, I don't know about that, but I'd like to meet your mom soon."

"We're from Mississippi. I'll tell her," Tammie said excitedly.

"Please do that. National Convention will be in Biloxi this year."

When I went to walk away again, my mom squeezed

my hand. I just stood there looking for a second. She was introducing me to ladies in the graduate chapter that were on the advisery council for Alpha chapter. Everyone was so nice, which was a big contrast to the Alpha chapter sorors themselves who were over in a corner, mad as a kid on Christmas with not one toy. But I wasn't Santa Claus or their parents, so I didn't care that they were upset. I was on the line, and they were gonna have to deal with it.

"Okay, look here." Tammie came up to me and handed me a note as my mom got caught up socializing. "We're meeting at this address in thirty minutes. Come with your two friends. We've gotta work out this whole line thing."

"Are the big sisters gonna be there?" I asked, wanting no part of any underground junk.

"It's just us. I told you I was gonna give you some inside information. Come, all right?"

"Oh, my gosh! I'm going to my first meeting," Torian said, all giddy in the car twenty minutes later. Loni and I were both skeptical.

"I'm just telling you now, if those big sisters are there, I'm gonna turn right around and leave," I said.

"I'm driving, so you'll be walking home," Torian said.

"No, I'm serious, Torian. I'm not planning to get caught up in all that. It's not why I want to be a Beta."

"You don't even know why you want to do it," she said. "Y'all just want to be paper."

"And what is paper?" I asked.

"When you go through not one part of hazing and automatically become a member of the sorority."

I leaned forward into the front seat and said, "Grand

chapter sets rules by laws and covenants; it's meaningful stuff. If it's good enough for them to say that's all you gotta do to be a Beta, it's good enough for me. I'm fine with paper. I'm just telling you, if there's any drama, I'm leaving. And if you got a problem with it, I'm taking your keys, or I'll walk home."

Torian gave in and lightly pushed my shoulders backward. "All right, all right, all right."

We arrived at the address and walked into a classroom in the science hall. No lights were on, except in the room we had stepped into. The seven girls on our line were there and stared at us like we'd done something awful. I knew I should have stayed at home. Shoot!

"The meeting started five minutes ago," said the girl who had stood right in front of me on the line.

"What's your name?" I asked her, already annoyed.

"I'm Jaden, and I already know you're Malloy. Come in. They're here, y'all. Okay, well, here's the bottom line," Jaden said as she ushered us in. "I'm not asking because I've been voted the Line President. If you want some respect and credibility, we're gonna have to haze you guys to get you up to speed on all we've been going through."

"Are you crazy?" I said without flinching. "Why would I let y'all touch me? I don't need your respect. Plus, I never voted you president."

Jaden smirked and said, "It was unanimous with the seven of us real pledges. We didn't need your vote for me to hold this position."

"No, I'm sorry. You guys aren't gonna touch me either," Loni said.

"Come on, guys, we can do this," Torian said in a desperate tone, trying to convince us.

"Girl, you can do this. I don't want nothing that bad, and I don't have to do this to get it." I turned around and walked toward the door.

"I'm Maxine. The Line Vice President. You walk out of here, and you're never coming back into the fold with us. We went through a lot and the seven of us have discussed it. You all need to go through something to be even with what we've done."

I kept walking.

"I'm talking to you," the Maxine girl said as she grabbed my hand.

I snatched it quickly away from her. "I have always known this sisterhood thing was something that wasn't even really obtainable. Some myth about a tight bond. You've just proven my point. You touch me ever again and the crap the Betas are putting you through will be nothing compared to the beat-down I'll give your tail."

I walked out, and Loni quickly followed. I was so angry. Those girls had some nerve. Loni turned around and said to Torian, "Come on. Malloy's right. They ain't gonna beat us up. This is crazy."

Torian came out reluctantly as Maxine said, "You guys just ostracized yourselves. You've made a huge mistake."

PREGNANT

"How can we grow and be a part of all they're doing if we're not in the mix?" Torian said to Loni and myself as we drove home from the private meeting with our line sisters that had gone nowhere. "I wanna go back."

"You driving back?" Loni asked like it was just okay with me if they turned the car around and went back and subjected themselves to torture. "I've thought about it. Torian has a point, Malloy." Loni tried rationalizing with me. "I mean, we wanna be a part of the sorority, but we don't wanna go through everything it takes to actually be in it. What's a little shove or a little verbal abuse gon' do? It's not gonna hurt me. It's not gonna break me. But if it's gonna make them respect me, it's fine. Come on."

"You guys take me home now," I demanded.

"I knew she wouldn't do it," Torian said under her breath.

"You guys shouldn't want to do it either. Bottom line, there is more than one way to do something. If y'all participate, who knows what'll happen? I'm sure you'll be in for more than you can handle."

"Well, Malloy, that's easy for you to say," Torian said as she pulled up to my apartment building. "Your mom is the National President. You don't have to go through everything to get your respect."

"Please, they treat me just like they treat you guys, and do you see me care?"

Loni said, "Not now, but I can see them coming around to you a lot more easily than they would to us."

"Well, my mom is not gonna be the National President forever."

Torian said, "Yeah, but by that time we'd be sorors in an alumnae chapter, graduated, and working on our careers or something. Nobody will care then."

"Exactly. So you'd rather go through whatever foolishness they want you to experience now, when in a few years it won't even matter? You can't even see the bigger picture. We're in this to make a difference to the community. And how can we do that with somebody beating us up? Especially from girls that don't even have their letters."

"I just don't think it's going to be like that," Torian said. "It's a lot of talk. You saw those girls—everybody looked fine. Nobody's been abused."

"Fine! Y'all go back." I got out of the car, and steam blew from both my ears. When I got to my door, I couldn't get my key out fast enough. I didn't know all my neighbors, but this big guy was walking in my direction. It was dark, so I couldn't see his face. Nervously I dropped my keys. When I picked them up, the body was in my space.

"It's me, babe, don't be scared," Kade said as he put his arms around my waist.

"Oh, my God, I was about to head inside, grab a lamp or something, and knock you over the head. Why didn't you tell me you were coming?"

"I didn't know how long you'd be with all that sorority stuff. Plus, I sent you a text."

We headed straight to my bed, and his kisses warmed my soul. I'd actually forgotten I was so upset. Girl drama was stressing me out. Kade was helping me unwind.

Breaking away from his embrace, I said, "You just don't know how much I needed this."

"I gotta confess. I need to be with you, too," he said.

I could feel the desire of how bad he wanted me coming from his every word. I sat up in the bed and held him. He hung his head low, and I knew he hadn't come all this way for sex. He needed a pep talk.

I stroked his head and asked, "What's going on with you?"

"I'm nervous about this game. I haven't been a hundred percent since I got hurt, and more scouts are coming to check me out. There's talk that I'm losing my step. I don't know. I mean, maybe I am."

It almost felt like I was holding my own baby. But I appreciated him needing me in a way I'd never seen before. He was so vulnerable, as though whatever I said could make or break his hopes and belief in himself. Knowing our bond was deepening, I said only what a girl wanting to uplift her man could say.

"Honey, you're the bomb. You gon' shine in whatever you do. So let the scouts come. They'll be in for a show."

He took both his hands and cupped my face, pulling my lips toward his. Everything at that point felt so good.

"I want you, but I just want to snuggle tonight," he said.

I knew that having Kade sleep over wasn't God's plan for my life. I mean, I wasn't married. Kade didn't see that coming anytime in the near future. But I knew the way my heart felt for him. So how could I refuse a cuddle?

I was on my way to my second gem ceremony that was to focus on sisterhood. The whole idea of it felt contrived. I actually felt a little sad, though I knew I had made the right decision not to participate in any of the hazing craziness that wasn't supposed to be happening in the first place. I was a loner. And though that was the way it had been most of my teen years, I was pledging a sorority, for goodness sake. Even though I didn't want to admit it to myself, part of me wanted to belong.

I liked the first gem ceremony we had had a few days before. The focus had been on leadership, and it moved me to want to be the best leader I could be and always work with what I had. I'd had no idea how this first gem ceremony would affect my soul.

The only time I had talked to or seen Loni and Torian the last two weeks had been when we were doing the things with the adviser. A part of me resented that they had pulled back, but like all my other friendships, they eventually ended. I didn't know why I had thought this time would be any different.

As we lined up to go to the ceremony, I smiled at Loni and Torian, and they looked away. If it was like that, I understood. I'd never make a gesture again.

Tammie came from the front of the line and sashayed her way over to one of the big sisters. After she whispered something to her, Tammie came over to me.

She whispered, "Your girls just wanted me to tell you they love you and they care about you, but they gotta keep it like this so the big sisters won't get on them. You're able to talk to me. I've been kissing big sisters' butts for three and a half years. I'm a senior. I know all their dirt, and I helped them all make it through the line. They owe me. I do what I want to do. You were looking a little sad, so I just wanted to tell you—"

"I'm not looking sad. I'm fine," I said, completely denouncing what I knew I was feeling.

The only instructions we'd had before coming here was to fast all day—the cleansing of the soul to get us ready to begin the richness of the gem. There weren't many alumnae sorors here. Only the main adviser and the Alpha chapter Betas.

The vibe in the room for me not sisterly. I got mean stares from the Betas. And one girl made a fist. Though I had several issues with Hayden, after everything she had gone through with her own line, I would have thought she would have been a by-the-books sort of girl. Now she was condoning an underground line. It was just hard to swallow. But she did have a presence about herself when she read for the ritual.

Putting aside the personal issues, listening to her words, I was mesmerized when Hayden said, "Sisterhood is a bond with your soror that is as deep as a natural birth connection. The common thread that keeps you together is that you share a love for Beta Gamma Pi. Though you may have your differences, or you may not see eye to eye and agree with a soror's action, you love her at all times because that genuine connection never fails. Sisterhood is an evolving process of growth."

The adviser stood and continued reading. "When you're going through hard times, and you don't know who to turn to, call your sister. When the pain just hurts, and it seems you can't bounce back, the one to call first is your sister. When you think no one will understand, go and get your sister's hand and tell your sister. Not only when you want to cry. Go get your sister so she can help you become new and fill you with love that will get you back afloat. Your sister is your greatest treasure."

Big sister Dena, who was under five-two, took a loaf of wheat bread and held it upward. She asked Tammie to take a piece. Then everyone in line after that took a piece of the loaf.

Hayden said, "As you all get nourished from the same grain, now your line is one."

As moving as all that was, an hour later I was home by myself. I knew they were having more underground stuff going on.

"Hey," I said to Sirena after I'd gotten her four text messages about asking me to come over to get some of her stew. She'd always make me a pot of this or bring me a plate of that. I knew the girl could throw down, and I guess I just needed the company. But it felt a little weird as she stared me down. Finally I had to ask, "What? What are you looking at?"

Swatting her hand at me, she said, "No, no, you're just so cute. I just wish I had style like that. That's all."

"Oh, girl, please. I wish I could cook like you," I said as I stuffed myself with her stew.

Then I heard banging outside. It seemed like it was coming from my place. Sirena rushed over to her front door and yelled, "She's not home!"

"Who is that?" I said, perplexed.

Without looking, Sirena said, "Ugh, it's late. Don't nobody need to be over at your house at this time."

Going over to the door myself, I said, "Girl, you can't make that call. I think someone is at my house."

"But we were eating."

"I'm sorry. I'll come back if I can. Dang." I opened up the door to leave.

"Oh, I—I—I'm sorry. I didn't mean to be pushy," Sirena said.

It was almost eerie how clingy she was becoming. But when I turned toward my front door, I was stunned. There stood Loni holding Torian, who was bleeding from her nose.

Knowing the answer already, I asked, "Who did this?"

"I left. I can't take anymore. They hit her. Bad," Loni said as I opened my door and went inside.

Why they had come to me for help, I didn't know. But something I wasn't familiar with kicked in, and I was genuinely concerned for my friend. I couldn't turn them away. Somehow we were going to figure this out. The Betas had lost their minds.

* * *

After we got Torian straight, I grabbed the keys out of Loni's hand. "Let's go."

"No, you can't say anything to them," Torian said, holding her head in the air.

I didn't turn around. This had gone too far. Just a little push here, just a little shove there. A few harsh words. Whatever. We'd just stopped blood from profusely streaming from her nose. We all got in Loni's ride, and I took off, thinking I'd find the Betas even if Loni didn't give me directions.

"The whole two weeks have just been way too much," Loni confessed. "I wanted to walk away so many times, but I stayed because Torian felt like we should."

I asked, "Who actually hit you? Was it Sharon?"

"Girl, we haven't even seen Sharon. Somebody said she's sick," Loni said in a salty tone.

"It was a couple girls from the University of Southeastern Arkansas and some beast named Keisha."

"So y'all were with their line?"

Loni said, "Yeah, we're supposed to be with their line next week, too. Turn right there."

"Don't tell her where to go," Torian said to Loni.

"No, this is crazy. They need to be stopped for real." We arrived and I got out of the car and went inside, Torian and Loni right behind me.

The room was scorching hot, and it wasn't summertime. It was funky in there as well. All the Betas were hovering over the pledges like they were about to beat them down.

I saw Dena and another girl named Audria. Forget big sisters and all that protocol junk, because they didn't have my respect and I wasn't going to pretend like it was there. I boldy said, "Where's Hayden?"

"She's not here," Dena said, rolling her eyes. I wanted to smash her for allowing my girl to get beat.

Taking a deep breath, I asked, "Does she know what y'all just did?"

Then this bigger, very mean-looking, unkept soror came over. "Oh, that's that paper girl y'all were talking about?"

Dena whispered to her, "Keisha, be cool."

"Yeah, I'm the one whose mom is the National President, so let me just say y'all keep hittin' people, and I'm gonna rat on this line. Nobody will cross."

Nobody was moving, and they looked like they thought I was bluffing. I pulled out my cell phone and started dialing my mom.

"Okay, y'all get away. Get out of here. She could call the adviser on us."

When the line dispersed, Tammie came over to me and said, "She wasn't supposed to get hit. Torian just said a few things out of line."

Torian said, "I told them not to hit anybody else. Look at the girl who stands two people in front of you. She has a black eye."

Sally was her name. When the big sisters piled out, Sally came over to me. Actually, all the hazed sisters huddled around me. I just knew they were going to go off on me for threatening to expose them. But I appreciated their surprising response when Sally cupped Torian's face and said, "Thanks for caring more about yourself. They are taking this thing too far."

"Why don't you just walk away?" I asked her.

"I guess I'm not strong enough. I wish I had some of your spirit."

"Well, go. Everybody, go home. Don't fool with them anymore tonight. We'll figure this whole thing out."

As though the night couldn't get any crazier, I was finally home resting when Kade called. "I'm at your front door. Let me in, please. I don't want that crazy neighbor of yours calling the cops."

"She's not that bad. You okay?"

"I need to talk to you. Please. I gotta get back to school."

"All right, all right. I'll be right there." When I let him in, his eyes looked swollen. "You been crying or something? It's not your leg. Did you get hurt again at practice?" I was getting all beside myself with worry because he wouldn't open up and talk to me. He had driven all the way to chat, but he wasn't saying anything. What was going on? "You wanna break up or something?"

"Why would you say that?"

"You're all distant and everything, I mean, what else am I supposed to suspect?"

"It's Sharon, okay?"

"You wanna get back with Sharon?"

"No. Just listen for a second. Please, Malloy."

"Well, talk to me, Kade. You come over here, and you're all worked up, and you think I'm not gonna be upset, when I clearly see you're distraught. What is going on with Sharon?"

"You must not have seen her lately."

"No, I told you I don't participate in all that under-ground stuff. Plus, word is she's sick. She hasn't been around in a while."

Putting his head against the wall, he mumbled, "She's sick, all right. She's ruining my life, that's what she's doing."

I touched his back. "How can she threaten you? What's going on?"

Kade turned to me with the saddest eyes I'd ever seen. "Malloy, I'm sorry, but Sharon's five months pregnant."

BREAK

"**G**et out!" I screamed at the top of my lungs, "Get out now, Kade! Go!"

My pillow was on my bed, and all I could easily grab, pick up, and throw at him was that limp object. I wished I had something heavier. I couldn't believe what he had just told me. Sharon pregnant? This was horrible. Were they even still involved? Had I still been sitting in the fool's chair all these months? I hadn't given him any in months, and he hadn't been pressing me. Was she satisfying him?

Coming toward me to try to convince me otherwise, he said, "No, no, you don't understand."

"What do you mean, I don't understand?" I huffed.

"I told you she's five months pregnant, Malloy. Think back. I haven't been with her since then."

I sat on the bed and actually started calculating it all. No way could I take his word for it. I hadn't seen Sharon around any of our legitimate pledge experiences, so that would at least account for why I didn't know she had a bulging tummy. Everyone else said she had been missing in action from the underground activities. Maybe this was why.

"So she's just telling you now?" I looked up. "I mean, if you're saying you haven't been with her, are you sure you're the dad?"

"Honestly, Malloy, I can't be sure of anything. But she's telling me I am, and she and I already agreed I'm getting a paternity test done. I wish she'd gotten rid of the baby, but five months . . . Now there's nothing I can do. We were together the week before I met you at that convention. I know I don't love her—even then it was just for sex. I know I don't want to have a future with her, but she sees dollar signs. When I cut it off, I guess she just decided she was just going to keep us connected in her own way and waited until it was too late to tell me. Gosh, I can't stand her."

I really couldn't stand her either for so many reasons, but now she was potentially carrying the child of a guy I really cared about, maybe even loved. I was scared to even think that. Now at least I knew why I couldn't let myself get so involved, and take things to the next level. Perfect timing, too. Just when my feelings were about to go there, go to that next level, go to that place where he'd have my heart totally, there I sat before him completely broken.

Now It seemed Kade wasn't even the one who had intentionally hurt me. I was beyond upset with myself. This was why I had to keep my heart in check and not get too close to him.

My dad had hurt me long ago by walking out on not just my mom but on me as well. My heart had been crushed, I had vowed never to get myself in a situation where I would feel like that again, but here I was.

Though I was tough and considered slightly hard, I did have a heart. And I knew I had to do what was right. I couldn't let Kade feel obligated to whatever we had. So I looked at him, a guy who clearly looked torn apart himself. Seeing the despair in his brow, I knew it wasn't easy for him to tell me all this, but he had. It was his reality. It was something we had to deal with. So I turned his cheek toward me and said, "You have to leave."

"I thought we just got past all that. I didn't mean for this to happen. This wasn't what I set out for."

Cupping his face with my hand so he knew I was sincere, I said, "No no, I understand all that, Kade, I do, but you're going to be a dad. You talked about that the first time I ever had a conversation with you. You told me you wanted to be a better father than the father you had, regardless of the circumstances and how it came about. No, this might not be ideal, but you're going to be a dad. Take care of this child. Make a family. Go be with Sharon. Work it out."

The tough football player, one of the best in college athletics, stood before me with tears in his eyes. He got down on both knees and placed his head on my waist. All I could do was rub his head and bend down and hold him. And though this was hurting me as much as I could clearly see it was hurting him, it was the right thing to do. If I was wrong, I had to be wrong doing something right.

"We got to cut this off. Please don't make this harder. Please leave." I went over to the door, and Kade grudgingly left.

It was now time for the Beta Gamma Pi Eagle Weekend. This was the overnight experience the line had with the alumnae sorors. This step in our ritual existed so the line could bond. I was so on the outs with everyone, I had no expectations that being one with the group was at all possible. But because this was a legit activity, and none of the Alpha chapter Betas would be there, I was in.

When I opened my door to look for my ride, Sirena came over and said, "You got your bags packed. Where are you going?"

"Just something with a sorority."

"I can't believe you're still fooling with those girls. Y'all are going away overnight? What are you all going to be doing?"

Squinting, I teased, "Girl, you are not my mama. Why are you getting all in my business?"

"I'm just asking," she said.

Loni and Torian told me Sirena was clingy. I tried not to see it because she was really cool and could mix up a mean jambalaya. I did need her to step back, stay in her place, and not get all up in my space. But I knew her, and the only way to ask this was to say, "Could you watch out for the place?" I needed to give her something to feel part of so she'd back off.

"Oh, yeah, I got that covered. I'll watch this place like a lion watches his prey," she said with her hard stance.

"Let's go, girl!" Tori shouted from her car window as she honked.

My mom had called and told me the Eagle Weekend was going to be something I would cherish because it was a time where we would all feel very close to one another. I had doubts, but as the three of us followed the map and drove for forty-five minute to a secluded day spa, I smiled because I loved getting pampered.

Torian, Loni, and I were isolated in the sorority. I really didn't care, but I could tell Torian especially wanted to make sure this was her weekend to blend in with our other line sisters. For the first part of the day, we introduced ourselves and met all the older alumnae ladies, but I was just going through the motions.

Eventually, it was spa time. I was in heaven. I needed the deep-tissue massage as a diversion from my woes. It had been five days since I'd kicked Kade out of my place. The two of us hadn't spoken since. And honestly I was hurting.

After dinner, it was time for our line to have confession time. I thought the girls in our line were a bunch of self-centered chicks that didn't know nothing about nothing, so I showed up in my pj's, ready to put on my headphones to listen to music. Astonishingly when we conducted the truth exercise, I was amazed at how deeply these girls had really connected to one another.

Cassie, the number three on our line, got up and said, "I just don't know how I would have made it without you girls. My grandmother's funeral was so hard for me to take. We didn't expect the cancer to take her so soon. If you guys hadn't been there, I don't know how I would have made it." Seeing the other seven of them break down in tears let me know their connection was superstrong.

Then Trencia, a full-figured girl, got up and said, "What Johnny did to me . . ." I started thinking, *What Johnny did to her? Now what happened?* "The whole rape ordeal was just way too much to bear. I wanted to brush it under the rug and pretend he didn't exist, blame myself, but you guys wouldn't let me. You all made sure I reported the incident, got myself checked and tested. I am so excited about the love we share. It's hard, but I know date rape is real."

Mulani, the cutest dark-skinned sister I'd ever seen, said, "And when my family was looking for a donor for my little cousin's dying body, y'all supported me when I wanted to get tested. As I went through the testing, I was scared, and some of you guys came to the hospital with me, and others took class notes I missed that day. It turned out mine wasn't a match. But I love y'all for having my back, and there's nothing I wouldn't do to make us closer. I just appreciate you guys."

There were more stories that were just as impactful; I couldn't believe I hadn't experienced all that with them. I was on line with these girls but completely separated from everything they had shared. In some ways, I wished I could have been there for them. I had thought it was all about the hazing, all just about the mental strife, but there was much more. It clearly was about sisterhood on a level I wanted, longed for, and needed. I had been distant for far too long.

Moved, I stood up and said, "All right, I know y'all have issues with me because I haven't gone through all the stuff you guys have gone through. But now that the alumnae ladies have gone to bed, I'm just going to keep it real. I really appreciate hearing all you have shared. I know you all have already bonded, but y'all don't need to go through anything extra with those crazy girls. Unify and tell them no more. I just felt I had to say that."

Cassie came over to me and said, "I don't really want to go through anything else, but we're in so deep, and they won't back down. We need help. You get special privileges because your mom is National President. We don't have that same nest to fall back on. You got to help us."

I got several looks that were different from the hard ones I'd gotten the night we became Pis. The girls looked tired and worn out. Like they truly hated they were being mentally and physically beat down.

Seeing uncertainty on my face, Cassie said, "You got to find a way to break us from all this."

"I'll try," I said, as we all hugged.

So much more bonding and talking went on that night that for the first time in a while, I was a happy to be a part of their group. Life was hard, but having people there to help you weather the storm was a blessing.

On Sunday evening, the Eagle Weekend was over. Torian, Loni, and I hated to leave, but an hour later, we were back at my place. We sat in the car and just talked about everything we had experienced that weekend.

"That was so moving, y'all," Torian said.

"Yeah, I'm glad to know everybody a little bit more," Loni confessed.

Torian said, "So, you know, Malloy, we really got to

try to stop this underground stuff. You've got to catch them in the act or something. We have to figure out some kind of way where they don't have to go through any of that."

"How am I supposed to catch them? I'm not following anyone." I looked at her like she was crazy.

Torian sighed like she really wanted me to hear her out. "Cassie said she would give me a call, she'd give me a text, she'd do something to let me know when they were doing underground stuff. When I get the word I just want to know you're going to be down. You're the only one who can make sure the hazng will stop and we can all still be Betas."

"I don't know if I can do anything like that."

"You've got more of a chance than we do," Torian said as Loni nodded.

I went inside and found five messages, none from Kade. Not that I expected him to go back on what I had forced him to do. But I did miss him so. The messages were all from Sirena, saying the house was cool, saying she was checking on me, wondering why I hadn't come back, hoping I'd come over for tea. She needed a life, and I couldn't call her now to check in, I was too tired. The weekend had been too draining. I had given so much that when my phone rang, I ignored it and drifted off to sleep.

"These girls better not be doing anything," I said out loud to myself as I picked up the ringing phone hours later. "Hello?"

"Girl, we're coming to get you."

"What are you talking about?"

"Cassie just texted us. They're out."

Frustrated, I said, "It's two in the morning."

"I know. They're driving the big sisters around, and they're doing something with the University of Southeastern Arkansas girls."

Mad that the Betas couldn't leave well enough I alone, I said, "Are you serious?"

"Yes. They want you to take some pictures and send it to your mom."

"All right, I'll be ready."

When we got in the car we drove to where Cassie had said they would be. It was an abandoned warehouse I'd never seen in my two years in the college town. There were over ten cars haphazardly parked around it.

At three ten in the morning, I eased up from the backseat and said, "This is crazy. I'm tired of spying. They are too grown to be putting up with stuff they don't want to do."

"Yeah, but you know it's just not that easy to tell them to stop. Malloy, you know nobody wants to be branded like the three of us are," Torian reminded.

"The three of us are smart. How about that?" I said to the two of them as I tapped them on the shoulders.

"Wait, I'm getting a text," Torian said as she reached for her ringing mobile. "Cassie says Keisha—I guess she got in trouble last year for doing so much on the line—has been drinking."

"Drinking?" Loni said.

"She says they're coming out to get something,"

All of a sudden, the door swung open, and four girls came swaggering out. The largest girl was waving keys around and couldn't even walk straight. And she was so loud we could hear her yelling at Cassie even with our windows up. I knew they were drunk.

"There's Sharon," I said.

It was wintertime, and she had on a coat, so my friends couldn't tell what was really going on. I knew there was a baby hidden in there. The fourth girl I remembered from Eagle Weekend; she was from the University of Southeastern Arkansas.

"Yep, there's that Keisha girl," Torian said, pointing to the larger girl.

Loni said, "You know everybody."

"Yeah, I tried to get to know them, thinking they would like me. I didn't know she was going to leave school because she put your girl Sharon in the hospital last year."

Offended, I hit her on the head and said, "Don't trip. She is not my girl."

We watched as they got in the car. Keisha was in the driver's seat. Sharon took the passenger seat. If Keisha was a fool and had severely harmed Sharon last year, why was Sharon with her? Why were they letting Keisha drive? People did stupid things.

"Where are they taking them now? How come everybody else isn't leaving? What should we do?" Torian asked in an uneasy tone.

"I don't know. Cassie is getting in the car with them." Loni stuck her head out the window to get a closer look. "Why do they have her hands all tied up? This is so crazy."

"Yeah, they're doing something foolish with her. Let's follow them," I said when they took off.

We tried to stay back, but Keisha was driving so fast,

Torian had to break the speed limit to catch her. No sooner had we thought they should slow down than Keisha veered off the road, and her car slammed into a tree.

Torian abruptly pulled over and started screaming. When I saw the car, I was in shock, too. It was practically wrapped around the tree. Four people were in there. Loni started shaking like she was having a panic attack. Seeing this horrendous scene, all three of us were about to break.

GRAVE

"Oh, my gosh, oh, my gosh!!" Torian continued to scream.

The three of us unlocked our car doors, and we ran over to the car. All we could see was blood, glass, and still bodies.

"Does someone have their phone? Hand me a phone!" I yelled, trying desperately to hold it together and get help. "We have to call the police!"

"I don't think they're going to be able to do something now," Loni said as she cried.

"Here, t—take mine." Torian handed it to me, clearly shaken and unable to talk.

"There has been an accident. Come quickly," I said to the 911 operator as I gave specific directions on where I thought we were and what we'd just witnessed.

"Any movement in the vehicle, ma'am?" the female operator asked me.

Thinking I'd see none, I quickly looked and was elated to be wrong. "Oh, my gosh! Somebody's moving! Come quickly, please! You got to come quick! There is movement in the back of the car. Please!"

The calm voice of the operator said, "Help is on the way."

The three of us joined hands and huddled together. Loni's tears got stronger. Torian looked as if she'd seen a ghost. We all were in shock and wanted to do something to help.

I immediately prayed. "Lord we need you right now. The folks in this car need a miracle, Lord. I know hazing and drinking and driving are wrong, but as college students, we make mistakes. We don't have it together. We need grace."

"Everybody needs to know what's going on. Everybody's got to know. We gotta go tell them!" Torian said, shouting.

Shaking her, I said, "Yeah, but somebody needs to stay here."

"I can't go anywhere. I can't leave," Loni said.

"It's okay. I'll go," I said, taking the keys from Torian. "Talk into the car. Let them know we're getting help."

I got back to the abandoned warehouse, and it seemed like there were more cars than before. The door was unlocked, and I didn't know if I should knock. I didn't have to be sweet; lives were hanging in the balance. When I stepped through the door, a Beta named Trisha came to the door with Bea. I saw Tammie positioned at the front of the line. I shook my head, and Tammie knew all wasn't great with Cassie.

Trisha took my collar and said, "What, so now you want to wake up and smell the coffee? You want a part of this? How did you know where we were, scrub?"

"First of all, you need to get your hands off me, and second of all, there was an accident." I jerked away.

Bea said, "What you mean, an accident? All of us are here."

"No, big sister!" Mulani shouted. "Big Sister Mean Machine Keisha and Cassie went to the twenty-four-hour Wal-Mart."

Trisha's eyes became large. "Keisha? She's been in an accident?"

Hating to deliver horrible news to anyone, I said, "It doesn't look good at all."

"My line sister Rose was with her!" Jackie said. I remembered her, she was a Beta from the University of Southeastern Arkansas who I'd met on my birthday.

Rose had been the girl I didn't know. So it appeared she was from the other college. This was hard. Now two schools were involved in this bad accident.

Bea said, "And Sharon is with her, too. She's pregnant!"

"What?" Trisha said.

This didn't shock me, but clearly everybody didn't know. Besides Kade telling me, no other word had gotten to me about it. Putting aside how I felt about her pregnancy, I could only pray she would walk away unhurt from the car accident.

"Where's Hayden?" I asked, knowing the highest chapter officer needed to be in on what was going on.

"Hayden never participated in any of this stuff," Trisha said as she paced back and forth.

I stood by Jackie and eyed Trisha seriously. "We need to call her. She's the president. She needs to be there."

"Uh-uh, she can't know," Trisha said. "Let's go, everybody."

"Maybe I wasn't clear about how bad things are. Police are on the way. What you're doing is illegal. Everyone doesn't need to come." I shook Trisha hard, trying to get her to understand that the accident was not really something everybody needed to come and see.

"Okay, I'll call Hayden, everybody else, stay here," Trisha said. "Bea and I will be back."

Trisha and Bea got in the car with me; they were so upset they couldn't drive either. I'd never seen the big sisters so on edge. I could only pray things would be better than when I'd left the scene. When we got there, there was an ambulance, fire truck, and three police cars. When I saw Torian being restrained by Loni and an officer, unable to be controlled and sick with grief, I knew the worst had occurred.

"Oh, my gosh, somebody's dead," Trisha said, taking in the horrific scene.

"How many people were in the car?" Bea asked.

"There was four of them," I said,

"Oh, my gosh! Oh, my gosh!" Bea collapsed as she saw the mangled steel that had used to be an automobile.

Loni spotted me and let Torian be held by the officer. She jogged over. I felt knots in my stomach.

"The girl from the University of Southeastern Arkansas is dead, Malloy," she cried as my arms held her. "We didn't see it, but she was ejected and thrown from the car. They found her body in the woods. They said she wasn't wearing a seatbelt, and the immediate death was caused by head injury and a broken neck."

"Oh, my gosh," Trisha said, grabbing her waist.

"Oh, no," I said.

"Not Rose!" Jackie cried.

I held Jackie tight. As bad as I felt, I knew Jackie felt ten times worse. I was so angry at this whole pledge process. Why they felt the old-school way was so important was beyond me. Now their crazy actions had cost someone their life.

"What about Sharon, Cassie, and Keisha?" I lifted Loni and asked.

After Loni collected herself, she said, "Keisha was driving, and she suffered a massive head injury. She is badly hurt. Sharon is, too."

Bea asked, "And the baby?"

"There's a baby? She's not even conscious. They don't know anything. They're just rushing them to the hospital. Cassie is the one they think is most out of danger."

Trisha, Bea, and I were happy for that.

"What have we done?" Bea said to a shaking Trisha as we saw the rescue workers carry a body with a sheet over it.

Trisha fell to her knees and shouted, "We were just trying to have a little fun, and now somebody's gone! Oh, God, forgive me!"

I had never seen somebody's body under a sheet. I've never seen a real crime scene or been involved in any type of horrific accident, but there I stood, watching the rescue workers. I felt numb. Maybe I shouldn't have let the four of them get in the car. Maybe I should have confronted Keisha and told her she didn't need to drive. I had clearly seen she was staggering. Because I was called to get some evidence to stop the hazing, I had wanted to catch the Betas doing something that would give my mom enough leverage to take over the line and stop the madness.

But I had known what was going on. Why hadn't I called my mom? Why hadn't I just ratted them out and told her what I knew? Then two police officers walked toward me. They started asking questions about Rose. "Officers, this was clearly an accident!" Trisha yelled after we could sense they were overly strong with us. "The driver herself isn't even available to tell you what happened. How do you expect any of us to know? We weren't here. We didn't see it."

"Young lady, calm down. Somebody called this in. We can trace the cell phone if we have to. Someone saw something." The officer looked at me as though I was holding back valuable information.

Not helping, Loni gave me a slight bump. Trisha couldn't even look my way. I knew I was supposed to speak up, but what was I supposed to say? On top of everything that had happened, we just needed to unite and get through this. I needed time to think. I needed to see if Keisha was going to survive before I went and put the blame on her. Plus, I held myself responsible. I should have stopped Keisha from driving. It just had all happened so fast. Finally I spoke. "Officer, we were driving home and saw a car lose control and crash into a tree."

"And who was in the car with you, ma'am?"

I pointed to Torian, who was still with the other officer, and then I pointed to Loni.

"Is that what happened?" he asked Loni.

She nodded.

"Well, let me get your information, and if we need to ask you anything further, we will at a later time."

"Sir, I just want to know . . ." Trisha said as she got really close to me, and then I smelled alcohol on her as well.

I pushed her backward. "She's doesn't have anything to say, officer."

"You ladies know each other?"

"Yeah, I know them," Trisha said.

"We're a part of the same sorority."

"Y'all need to be careful out here. It's a windy road, and it's dark. It's too dark for college students to be out at night."

Cassie got into an ambulance, and I panicked. "Wait, what's going on? I thought she was going to be okay. Why are they taking her away?"

The softening officer said, "They're going to take her in for precautionary measures to get her checked out to make sure she doesn't have any internal bleeding or broken bones."

An hour later, we were at the hospital. Hayden came up to me, and I'd never seen her face look so distorted. She had apparently been crying for a long while, and her eyes were puffy, her cheeks red. She ended up in my arms. "Thank you," she said.

"What? I should have stopped them. Why are you thanking me?"

"You tried to do what I couldn't. I just stayed away. Sharon told me all of it. You told Kade to get back together with her."

Caught off guard, I asked, "She told you that?"

"She's so happy about it. She hadn't been doing anything the whole pledge process, and tonight I guess she just wanted to be around. It might cost her everything."

I turned away. I hadn't heard from Kade, so it only made sense that he was working things out with Sharon. *Good for them,* I thought, remembering she was clinging to her life.

Hayden turned my discouraged face back to hers. "But listen. He still wasn't feeling it."

"What do you mean?"

"They weren't going to get back together. Sharon was trying to take her mind off that, but she was happy you tried for her. I honestly don't think she's ready to give up, but . . ."

A woman suddenly came from the ER, screaming, "I been in this hospital before, and my daughter almost didn't survive then! Now, fooling with this crazy hazing stuff, my grandchild is dead! Somebody's going to pay!"

Hayden started crying again after hearing the news. "Oh, no, Sharon lost her baby."

I could only hold on to Hayden. I had no answers. We were told that Sharon had had to have an emergency C-section, but it had been too late to save the baby. I couldn't make anything better, but I could be there for Sharon. I hoped it would a difference.

I had to call Kade. He had to know what was going on. Before I could call him, though, my phone rang. "Kade?"

"No, this is your mother. Why haven't you called me, girl, and let me know what in the world is happening with those Betas over there on your campus? I'm getting calls at all hours about some car accident. Please tell me this is a joke."

"No, Mom," I said in a somber tone. "Far from a joke."

"And you were out there? You were on the scene? If any underground stuff is going on, I know you'd be smart enough not to participate in any of it. Plus, I thought they weren't doing anything crazy. I mean, you had given me your word."

"No, Mama, I didn't give you my word that they weren't doing anything. I told you *I* wasn't."

"Then why were you out there, Malloy?"

"Because the girls on the line . . ."

Then I thought about what I was saying. I didn't know how all this needed to spin out. I didn't know what I needed to do to protect my fellow line sisters from all the craziness they had been through. Though I disagreed with it whole-heartedly, this was going to be more than anyone had to endure. Why should they have to pay the price twice?

Playing it safe, I said, "Mom, it's just crazy here right now. We got to talk later."

"Baby, please tell me are you're okay. I need to know the facts." I knew my mom couldn't sleep unless I assured her.

"Yes, I'm fine, but a Beta is dead."

"Oh, no! Malloy, are you serious? As parents we send you guys to school hoping you'll make right choices, putting you in organizations that believe in something, and you guys get together and just lose your mind."

"Two other girls are in critical condition right now. One of them was pregnant and lost her baby."

"Goodness. All right, I can't come up there as the National President, in case there are any legal issues. If someone sues our organization, I need to know as little as possible now. But I'm on standby as your mother. You need me, you call me right away. I'm going to make sure the Regional Coordinator is there. This is horrible. God be with us all and that precious young girl that's with Him now. I love you, Malloy."

"I love you, too, Mom."

As soon as I hung up, I called Kade.

"Yeah?" he said in a rocky tone.

"I know this will be a little weird, but I need to talk to you."

He perked up. "Malloy—hey, babe. What's up?"

"There's been a terrible accident, Kade."

"You all right?"

"No, it wasn't me. It was Sharon and some of the other Betas. The car ran off the road and hit a tree."

"What?" he said, really concerned. "How's she doing? She's all right?"

I started getting choked up as I found the words to talk about all this. Though Hayden had said Kade wasn't trying to get with Sharon, he hadn't reached out to me. Maybe he had been trying to take the daddy stuff in and then get with Sharon.

"Malloy, tell me, is she okay?"

"We don't know right now. She's in intensive care." I sighed. "But she has lost the baby."

"What?"

There was silence. I didn't want to pry, but I needed to know what he was thinking. So I asked.

"I honestly feel bad that I'm relieved a little," he said. There was silence again. "I wasn't trying to be no father, I tried to tell you that. You pushing me away didn't make me go into her arms. I'm not saying she trapped me or whatever, but she told me she was on birth control when we were together. For her to get pregnant, I don't know, I guess I should have used protection anyway. But make no mistake about it, I want her to be okay. I'm just numb about a baby I didn't want."

This was hard. How could I blame him for not being overly sad? We talked some more, and we prayed for Sharon. Then I got off the phone to be with my sisters.

I looked all around the emergency room and saw so many sad faces, such high emotions. This accident had ripped us apart, but Cassie was okay. We found out she did have a couple broken fingers and some deep bruises. However, we still didn't know how Keisha and Sharon were faring.

What we did know was that the Beta from the University of Southeastern Arkansas was gone, and Sharon's baby, too. This accident had been more than severe. It had damaged a part of us we could never get back. As I looked around the room, I saw through the sadness to the bonding I was a part of. Just when we were about to find hope in each other, the doctor came out and announced the driver's situation.

To over forty of us from my chapter and the University of Southeastern Arkansas chapter waiting, the doctor said, "I'm sorry, it's grave."

PRESENT

"Grave? What do you mean, grave?" Hayden asked amidst all the sobs.

We hadn't been one unit—the pledges and big sisters. However, at that moment we *were* a unit. Girls were sitting in each other's laps and holding hands. I was in the back, so I didn't know how or when they had all arrived, but all the faces were weary and broken. We weren't going home, though. We certainly were forced to see each other through this.

"Keisha's just come out of surgery, and for the next twenty-four hours, we'll have to see if she comes through on her own. The other young lady, Sharon, has come around. She's resting. Of course she's devastated. Personally she has asked to see a couple of you guys, but her mom is in there with her now. Depending on what her mom says, she really may need a couple of you to give her comfort after dealing with her tremendous loss."

Cassie came out of the emergency room, and we all got up and gathered around her. Just to see one person walking from the accident was a miracle.

"Thank you guys for caring about me. I have never been so terrified in my life. I didn't want Keisha to drive, but she told me she had it. And now they're telling me she might not make it. This is a lot, y'all. This is a lot. Malloy, Loni, Torian . . . where are you?"

"We're right here," I said, and girls made way for the three of us to get to her.

"Thank you three. I should have had the guts to step up and stand up. I should have taken a more active role. I'm the Line Vice President, and I let everybody down."

"It's okay, it's okay," I said as I held her.

She then went over to get hugs and encouragement from everyone else. Loni and Torian were so happy. Hayden pulled me to the side and said, "Sharon's mom said I can go talk to her for a second. I just wanted to let you know in case anybody is looking for me."

"I want to go, too," I said.

"I don't understand. You hate Sharon."

"Sharon just lost her baby. I don't know, I want to let her know I care."

Hayden put her arm around my shoulder, and we walked into Sharon's room.

"I guess I owe you a bit of thanks," Sharon said grudgingly.

"I don't understand."

"They told me you acted quickly. Had we been there

any longer, if I hadn't gotten to the hospital sooner, not only would I have lost my baby, but I would have been gone, too."

She looked weary and had bruises and cuts on her face and arms. I rushed over to her side and held her hand. I was so thankful she was okay. I just remembered the mangled car. God had given her back to us.

"You talked to Kade already?" she asked.

"What?" I said, trying to play it off.

"I said, have you talked to him? I'm sure you did. I bet he's not too sad that the baby is gone, huh?"

"He wasn't ready to be a father, Sharon, but I have told him that you're okay, and that was his main concern."

"How am I ever going to be okay? My baby's gone."

Hayden came closer. "You'll have plenty of time to have another baby when you get married, girl. Have a family and be able to take care of the child. Maybe this was just God's way of saying—"

Clearly upset, Sharon interrupted. "Don't even put God in this. The only thing He's saying to me right now is that I'm such a horrible person I don't even deserve to be a mom. That's why he took away my baby."

"Okay, let's not even look at any of this like that. God spared your life. That's a blessing, Sharon. Don't get worked up. You're still weak," I told her.

"I ain't got no beef with you, Malloy. Not only did you help save my life, but you tried to get Kade and I back to-gether. He told me the whole thing. Got mad props for you, girl. I love him, though, and I do plan to keep fight-ing for him. If you feel bad for me, stay away."

Not knowing what I would say, Hayden put her finger

over her mouth, telling me to keep quiet. I was so torn. I cared for Kade as well. I was not prepared to make Sharon any promises I couldn't keep. Then she moaned out in pain. Boy, this was hard.

Before I could walk out, she said, "The police want to question me about what happened. I had bad heartburn, you guys. I needed some Tums, and we were just going to the store to pick up a few things. That's all. I was too tired to drive. Is Keisha going to make it?"

"Right now we're just glad you pulled through. We're going to keep praying for her, okay?" I squeezed Sharon's hand.

"When it all comes down to it, us Betas really stick together. Thanks, Malloy, and I really want you to be my sorority sister. After you peel back all them layers, you got a real big heart. And I'm glad I was able to wake up and tell you that right here, right now. You know I'm thankful for you. Thanks for giving Kade and I another chance. He and I are going to make it."

I nodded, trying not to fuss with her about Kade. This night was about keeping her upbeat. I was understanding what sisterhood was all about. I smiled, and she felt peace.

A week and a half had passed, and it was a long one. We'd attended Rose's memorial service. It was packed. Keisha had also pulled through, but she was still in the hospital recovering. Sharon was back home with her mom in Texas, and I was rushing to get ready for finals because we'd spent the last days going through the other three gem ceremonies and studying to pass the Beta Gamma Pi exam. Everyone thought we did well on it.

One day, Sirena came over to my apartment and said, "Girl, you look very nice today."

In a somber tone, I said, "Thanks. I made this dress."

Sirena said, "Really? You got skills. Listen, I seen in the papers that you were some big hero, calling in that accident right away. You got to come over for dinner tonight. Girl, I'm making my jambalaya."

"Your jambalaya?" I said, finally getting excited for the first time in a while. "What time?"

"It's still brewing, but it's been on all night. It should be ready to eat in a few hours."

"Cool. All right, I'll be over."

She gave me a hug but didn't let go right away.

"All right, now that you're chokin' me, I'm not going to be able to eat nothing later on," I said, playing it off as I pushed her away. "All right, I'll see you later."

When I shut the door, the phone rang, and it was Hayden. "We need you to meet us on campus at the sorority room in an hour. Please come dressed in a black dress."

As soon as I got off the phone, Torian called. "You know we're going to cross tonight? We will finally be Betas."

"You think?" I asked.

"Yes, girl, we got to wear our black dress. We been through all the gem ceremonies. We had the Eagle Weekend. What else is there for us to do?"

"Yeah, because we even took the test, and, obviously, that is all that can be next."

"We're crossing tonight!" Torian screamed.

When we got there, we were all in the sorority room, and Jaden said, "We started out this line as two distinctly different sets. But today I stand in this room excited that this line is one. Malloy, Torian, and Loni, the three of you guys are all a part of us. The bonding experience has been successful."

Torian said, "I wanted to be a part of this group because of the sisterhood for so long. I wanted you guys to really want the three of us to be included in your heart. What I feel is real. I hurt when you hurt. I'm excited when good things happen to you. In every sense of the word I am your sister, and if this is our time, if we cross the burning sands, if we go from not being Greek to being Greek, let us take all that we've learned and be better. Let us continue to change and make the world awesome. Let us continue making each other even more dynamic."

People were sobbing, people were clapping. It was just the ten of us, but it was a special time.

Loni stepped up, grabbed my hand, and said, "This bond just . . . is deep for me. I got a lot of sisters, and I'm not as close to them as I am to some of you. Know that I'm here for you. If you need me, I'll give you the shirt off my back. We've endured some tough times, but I know we're stronger because of it."

Hayden looked over at me, and I had to be honest. "You guys, know I wasn't really feeling the whole sisterhood thing. I used to think this was something my mom forced on me, and I always resented her for not being there for me. However, somewhere along the way throughout this process, I finally figured out what's been keeping her from being my mom. I also realized and regret that I've been a little selfish. When you care so deeply about your sisters, as if they were family, and you feel and care so much for them, it's a bond that's a gift from God. Thanks for accepting me. Thanks for changing me. Thanks for showing me what love is. I appreciate what we have. I'm your sister."

Though I felt that in my heart, an hour later in the historic chapter room, we actually became sorority sisters. Over thirty alumnae and collegiate sorors made us members of their Beta Gamma Pi. My mother was a presiding officer, and it was an emotional ceremony. To put a high note on all we had endured, we knew that, becoming Betas came with a high calling. This vow the ten of us made was something we would never take for granted.

My mother came over to me and held me tight. I felt so honored. I was in the grip of my National President's arms. She kissed my forehead and would not let me go.

"Malloy, I love you so much. I'm proud to have you as my sister, but forgive me for not always knowing how to be your mom," she said with tears in her eyes.

Wiping them, I said, "You've had much on your hands that I didn't understand. I thought being so involved with BGP was a job. I now see it is a calling given to you by God. Forgive me for being so needy. I never went without. You were there for me every night. If I wasn't so selfish, I would have probably freed your heart to do even more good for Him and for our sorors."

"You saying this to me means more than you know. Thank you, baby. Your godmother wanted to be here; she'd be so proud of us right now," she said as she lifted her head toward Heaven. "Thank you, God. We get what the other needs."

* * *

When I got home after celebrating that night with my mom and new sorors, I was wiped out and ready to hit the bed. However, Sirena was at my door with her arms folded.

"What's wrong with you?" I said.

"We had a date. You were coming over for dinner, and you didn't even call. You didn't even show up."

"Oh, my gosh, I forgot," I said, knowing she would forgive me when she knew me and my line sisters had crossed. I showed her my letters on the back of my new T-shirt.

"Like I care about any of that."

"Okay," I said, stepping over her and taking out my key. "You stay on your side, I'll stay on mine. You can't understand that, then, girl, you need to get a life."

I went into my apartment and went about my business. Thankfully through all I had endured, I still had been able to maintain my grades. The semester was almost over, and I knew I'd do well on my exams. I was happy to be heading home soon.

I became a little melancholy and decided to call Jackie. I wanted to find out how the Betas at the University of Southeastern Arkansas were doing since they'd lost their chapter soror.

"Honestly, Malloy, it's so hard. Some of us still want to call her. Some are so happy that Keisha is okay; some want her in jail. I just don't think all this is over. Thanks for holding me down that night."

"No problem. I just wanted you guys to know we're sorry all this happened."

I hadn't known Rose at all, but to be at her service and hear what type of girl she had been, how much everybody cared about all she'd done, made me know Heaven was richer now that she was there. Jackie and I talked about that a little more, and I tried to give words of comfort. Then she congratulated me on crossing. "You going to our bowl game?"

"I'm sure my mom is going to make me go to support my brother. I can't believe they're playing in the big NCAA Division I Bowl."

"Yep, we're headed to New Orleans, baby, for the Sugar Bowl. I'll see you down there then."

"Cool."

A week later, it was Christmas. The day was great. My dad and brother came over for a big meal. We weren't a typical family, but we made the best of it. I wanted to let my parents know how much I cared about them doing so much for me. Though they had hurt me in the past, I knew it wasn't intentional. Plus, life was short. No day was promised. If I wanted things to change or to be different, I had to be the one to take a stand and make that happen. Being in a sorority had taught me a lot. It taught me not only to care about myself but to be proactive in wanting change.

So I said to my family at Christmas dinner, "This is really nice, the four of us sitting around at the dinner table together. Mom, Dad, you guys have given me and Mikey so much. Financially we are set. Maybe we don't say thanks often enough. I'm letting you know how appreciative we really are. I guess I just want to do better and make you proud. And I want us to spend more time together like this."

As I kissed my father on the cheek, he said, "That's a

good present to give your dad. Hey, maybe you and Mom will come to New Orleans and check out your brother and the Razorbacks in the game. Kade came up to me and asked if you were going to be there."

"Are you serious, Dad?" I said.

"Yeah. For him to talk to your pops, he's got to think something of you, because I looked him in the eyes and let him know straight up I don't play. He knows my baby don't need his money. Even if it is gonna be many times mine."

"I'll take it," Mikey joked. "For real, he likes you, and I'm actually pretty impressed. You didn't just give him everything he wants like every other girl he's come across. Malloy, you're pretty special. I'm letting you know his feelings are real. I wouldn't tell you that if I thought he was planning to hurt you. Now, I'm not saying he's going to be perfect, and I'm not saying he won't let you down, but he won't let up. Every time I see him, he's not talking about any game strategies, he is asking about my sister."

"Crazy," I said, not knowing what to think about Kade.

Six days later we were excited that Arkansas beat Michigan in the Sugar Bowl. I was waiting with all the other parents and friends for my brother to come out. Girls were looking me up and down. I knew word was I was Kade's girl. They didn't have to cut me with their eyes though. He and I were through.

Kade's mom came over to me and said, "Honey, my son is a special young man, and I don't want just anybody in his life. I know y'all are young, but I believe he deserves only the best and classiest young lady in his life. Whatever he did wrong, give him a second chance. He needs you."

I turned around, and he was standing right there looking better than I could have imagined. He was the MVP of the game, and that honor usually went to offensive players. I tried as hard as I could to hold back the desire I was feeling for him.

Then he looked right at me and said, "Tell me you'll give me another chance."

BASKET CASE

In front of his mom and my parents, Kade let out his feelings for me. I tried to act as if I hadn't missed him over the last few weeks. Like I didn't care that we weren't going to be a couple anymore and he hadn't put one hand on me, but I could feel his presence consuming every inch of my body and soon I was overcome with emotion.

"You don't have to cry," he said. "This is a good thing, and I'm not trying to go nowhere. Trust what I'm saying, I'm for real."

My dad leaned over to him and said, "We're staying at the Marriot. We'll make sure your mom gets to her hotel. You take care of my daughter. Y'all, talk. But I expect to see her at twelve o'clock."

"Yes, sir, twelve," Kade said, shaking my dad's hand.

"Good game." My dad said and then looked at me. "Malloy, is that all right with you?"

I could only nod, not wanting anyone to see the tears welling up in my eyes. I did care for Kade, but my soror Sharon cared for him deeply as well. How could I go down this bumpy road again? Regardless of my feelings, I walked with him.

New Orleans was still recovering from Hurricane Katrina, but the renovated Superdome was lovely. Although it was the last day of December, it wasn't that cold down South, so we were able to walk back to all the festivities and enjoy the University of Southeastern Arkansas' victory.

"So, we're been together for about fifteen minutes. You're not talking to me. I know you're thinking something, Malloy. I'm not trying to scare you, but I love you."

"You can't tell me that, okay?"

"What? You don't want me to love you?"

"I don't know. It's just—"

"It's just what? Open up. Talk to me. Tell me what's going on."

"Well, I thought you loved Sharon at one point. Now all of a sudden when someone else came on the scene, what you felt for her flew out the window. We're sisters now, and all this is so sensitive. I know she still loves you. She and I are cool now, but if I get back together with you, it's gonna add more drama."

"I hear you on the sorority thing because I have that type of deep bond with my teammates. I know it's real, and I know there are certain lines you don't cross. The sister bond is strong, but you and I were together before you got letters, and if you remember when I first met you, I had a girlfriend I was going to break up with. It wasn't some fly-by-night decision. I decided to end things with her and be with you. Now that there ain't no baby standing in our way, we can be together. Sharon's been told over and over again that we're through. I just want you." He eased closer to me. How could I pull away and deny the best connection I'd ever felt? I didn't realize I was trembling until Kade pulled me to him and said, "You cold?"

Looking away, I said, "I guess I'm just nervous, Kade."

"Well, how about this? Let me calm you," And he put his lips to mine, warming me from the inside out.

That kiss truly confirmed that I was his girl. There wasn't passion alone in his kiss, but so much more. When he stepped away, I thought I would fall down. That's how much he had me off balance.

He must've thought I was crazy when I lost it and said, "I just don't know if I can do it. I just don't know if I can give you my heart and have you stomp on it. Everywhere I went this weekend, some girl was talking to her crew about wanting to get with you. You're gonna be a number-one draft pick. I know that in my heart. Kade, you are so talented. Why do you even want me? You'll have it all."

He took me in his arms and placed a soft kiss on my forehead and said, "I won't have it all till I have you. Malloy, you are priceless. Love me back. I know you have your own dreams. You want to be a big fashion designer. I'm behind you, baby. I'm waiting for the day we see your name in lights."

I was so confused. I had no idea what to do.

* * *

When I got back to my apartment after winter break, I was ready to start the new semester. I was so excited to get back to my own space. My dad had bought me a new comforter set, and my mother had gotten me a whole new bath set. I was going to give my apartment a makeover.

Kade hadn't let up since New Orleans. He'd sent roses to my mom's place. He'd texted me so much with sweet messages that my inbox was full before I could check every one of them.

He was planning to come visit before he started all the training for the Senior Bowl and the NFL Combine—two big events that would help him show the pro scouts what a great athlete he was. I wanted everything to be perfect for our time together. Deep down I knew I couldn't stop my heart from wanting to be with this guy.

Yet my dream was shattered when I opened the door and found my place ransacked. The cloth furniture had been ripped with a knife, and there was spray paint all over the walls spelling disgusting words my mom always told me I was never to call myself—or anyone else, for that matter. The lamps were thrown here and there, all my dishes were broken into a million pieces, and my bedroom was more of the same.

Seeing it all shot chills up and down my spine. I was mortified. This was crazy. Who would do this to me? Who would take me through such torture, and for what? I picked up the phone but could not get a dial tone. I looked at the cord; it was cut.

I just fell to my knees and cried, "Lord, why is this happening? Is the person coming back? Please give me some clarity. Give me some answers. Help me." I ran out and knocked next door. I really needed Sirena. She'd know what to do. She'd help keep me calm, but apparently she wasn't back from Christmas break.

I dashed to my car, frantically searching for my cell phone. Finally I got it and called Torian. "Hey, please tell me you're back."

"Yeah, girl, I'm back. I was just hanging out with Trisha and Sharon."

"Sharon? What—what do you mean, Sharon? I thought she went home to Texas?"

"Nope. She's back this semester. She was here all Christmas break," Torian said before she whispered into the receiver. "She's real upset that you and Kade are back together.

Instantly I ran back into my house and looked at the graffiti on the wall. *Dream killer. Family wrecker. Hope slasher* were the only words that made sense. This had to be Sharon. She had ransacked my place!

"You gotta get over here quick!" I said to Torian.

"What? What's going on?"

"Somebody broke into my apartment. Torian, it's pretty bad. Get Loni. My stuff is everywhere. Help me figure this thing out. Hurry."

I was waiting at the front door for their arrival. They were there in twenty minutes, but it seemed to take forever.

"Oh, my goodnes! This is crazy! Who would do this?" Loni said as she looked through my apartment.

In anger, I responded, "It's Sharon."

"No, Sharon did not do this," Torian said.

"Yes, it's Sharon. I want to call an emergency meeting with the whole sorority. I want her to admit to me that she did this. She's gonna be responsible. I've called the police."

Torian said, "You can't tell the police she did this. If she did it, we gotta handle this in house. You know how we roll. We don't rat each other out."

"Look at my place! Look all around here! My life is destroyed. She's that crazy, she's that obsessed, she's that ticked that Kade does not want to work things out. Maybe she needs to cool off in the pen. Give me Trisha's number. She's there, right?"

"No, I'm not giving you Trisha's number. Y'all aren't gonna yell and scream and fuss all over again. Let's calm down and try to figure this out."

"Give me the doggone number now!" I screamed. "You know what? I got Hayden's number. I don't even need your help. If you ain't gonna be there for me, get out!"

"I'm just saying you don't even know if she really did it, and you all talking about trying to start World War Three in our sorority. We just came out of a whole bunch of mess, Malloy. That's all I'm saying."

"Look around—it's a bigger mess now, so you gotta take sides, Torian. You gotta decide if you're down for me or if you're going to stand with Sharon and think that her crazy actions are justifiable. Yeah, she lost her baby; yeah, she lost her man; but you know what? She can't just take it out on Malloy Murray. She cannot wreck my life. That's not cool!"

Torian came over to me, touched my shoulder, and said, "Okay, okay, you need to calm down. We'll get this figured out."

I shoved her away. "Don't tell me to calm down! This isn't your life that's screwed!"

"All right, y'all, settle down," Loni said. "Malloy, you know we're with you, right? Torian, tell her."

Reluctantly Torian nodded. I walked away from them both. They followed and stared at me with genuine concern. "Can y'all help me get to the bottom of this? Help me make Sharon pay."

They nodded again. We hugged. I called my folks and convinced them I was fine. I told them I was staying with Torian and Loni for a while. I knew my mom could hear in my voice that I was rattled. I didn't think I would be fine until Sharon paid for what she'd done.

I left Kade many messages. I knew he was training, but this was important. When I needed him, I needed him to be able to pick up. I was frantic that I couldn't. After the police came, I answered all their questions, including who I thought did this, and they filed a report. After, I went to stay with Torian and Loni.

"Okay, Trisha just called me back," Torian said as she hung up her cell. "She says Sharon doesn't want to come over and that she emphatically denies doing anything to your place."

Grunting, I said, "Of course she's gonna deny it. Why would she admit anything? Her butt's gonna have to go to jail. They're dusting my place right now for fingerprints. Call her up now and tell her that."

"Didn't you just hear me say she didn't do it?" Torian said as Loni handed me a glass of water. "Well, I was with her. She did not seem like someone who had just committed a crime. She was upset about Kade, but not enough to harm you. Heck, he cares about you. Don't worry about your place getting messed up. You can replace it all. You got loot, plus your man is about to make millions of dollars. Give it up."

"Are you kidding? It's probably gonna cost five grand to fix the damage she's done. And I am not paying for it."

I was so angry at them. Loni was quiet, but I knew as she nodded in agreement with all of Torian's statements that she wasn't really on my side. My cell rang, and it was my brother.

"Mikey, my place is trashed."

"Yeah, Mom told me. You don't need to stay over there."

"No, I'm with my girls. I'm just trying to get in touch with Kade. His crazy ex did this."

"Are you sure?"

"Why are you gonna question me?"

"I'm just asking. Dang! But you're right, she could have done this. Kade did say she was crazy. And to some people, being with him is like hitting the lottery."

Relieved someone could feel me, I said, "Speaking of Kade, have you seen him?"

"Naw, he wasn't at practice."

"What do you mean he wasn't at practice? He's supposed to come here after practice." I just hung up the phone and started pacing back and forth. Where was Kade? Why wasn't he answering his cell phone? What was he doing that wasn't right? Was he cheating on me? Oh, I was absolutely losing it. I had never been so fragile where a guy was concerned.

"You are not acting like a Beta." Loni said. "Don't let a man or whoever did this to your place control how you respond to what's going on right now."

Sighing, I said, "Okay, you're right."

"And if Sharon said she didn't do it, as Betas we gotta find it in our hearts to believe that's true."

"Are you kidding me, Loni? Are you joking?" I was hot again. "No way! Just because it's a sisterhood, I'm supposed to believe none of us lie? Bye, y'all."

"Where you going?" Torian asked.

"I'm not staying in here with y'all." I slammed their door, hurt that my buddies really were not on my side.

I drove back over to my place, and was happy to see Sirena's car. I guessed she was back after all, so I knocked on her door.

"Oh, thank goodness you're here, Sirena. Somebody trashed my place, and I can't stay there."

"I saw cops and stuff earlier when I pulled in. What happened?"

"I don't know, and I don't know where to go."

"Well, you know you can stay with me until your place gets fixed. I have only the one bed, but we can share it. Tomorrow I'll even help you clean up over there." She touched my arm, and I wasn't sure if I was still shaken up because of my apartment, but she made me feel uncomfortable.

Before it got any worse, I saw Kade's car speed into the parking lot. Sirena still tried to get me to go into her place, but I told her I had to talk to him.

He got out of the car and reached my front door. "Hey,

The Way We Roll 149

babe. I got your messages. What happened to your apartment?"

Angry, I asked, "Where've you been?"

"I thought you were coming in?" Sirena said.

"It's my boyfriend, girl. I'll knock a little later. I'm just trying to deal with him."

"Well, let me tell him that you don't appreciate him coming over so late."

"Sirena, thanks, but I can handle my man." I rolled my eyes at her, glad that Kade had come at the right time. She was so pushy.

She slammed the door, as he tugged me over to his chest. "I'm sorry. I was meeting with a couple agents. I had my cell off."

"Oh." I felt relieved and hugged him.

We walked into my place, and I showed him the damage. Kade was so mad. How could I have ever doubted him?

"I can sign with an agent, and he can front me money if we need to get your place fixed. I just can't believe Sharon would stoop so low and do this."

"You do believe me? You do think she did it?" I smiled when he nodded. "My dad is working on getting the place fixed. Thanks, though. I just want Sharon to pay."

"Yeah, the girl used to leave me so many desperate messages, I know she's crazy. When I told her it was over, she wasn't getting it. I can't believe she's tripping like this."

"Oh, Kade. What am I gonna do?"

"You're not gonna worry. I know that."

In my trashed place, I rested my head on his shoulder. For the first time in twenty–four hours, I was calm. I was no longer a basket case.

GIVE

"Where are you going to stay?" Kade said, kissing my brow.

"I don't know. I just can't believe this is happening."

"I'd give you the shirt off my back, even though you can make your own," he said, trying to make me smile, "but you know we can't have females in our dorms."

We walked through and completely assessed the damages to my place. Kade still couldn't believe that all this had happened, but before we could discuss Sharon further, someone knocked on the door. I was so startled by the door he had to grab me. "It's okay, it's okay. Your sorority sisters are here."

I turned around, not even knowing how to respond, seeing Torian and Loni at the door. I was upset with them. They hadn't taken my side. What in the world were they doing back at my place?

"We're so glad to find you," Torian said as she came over and gave me a big hug. "We were only saying that we didn't want to accuse Sharon so soon. We didn't want to put the verdict out and convict the girl. But we love you and care about you. Malloy, you have got to stay at our place."

"No, it's all right," I said, not wanting to be a burden on anybody.

"For real, where are you going to stay? The girl next door is weird," Kade reminded everyone.

"And you're our girl," Loni said. "Plus, I agree that girl next door is crazy."

Kade took my hand. "Mmmm, no way, you ain't staying with her. Let's get your stuff so you can stay with your sorority sisters. I'd feel more comfortable knowing they got your back."

"We'll take care of her," Torian said.

"I'm all right. I don't need anyone taking care of me," I responded, still shaking.

"Sometimes you just got to let go and let people in," Loni said.

"Yeah, you're always there for us. Whatever we need, we can count on you. Let us return the favor," Tori said as she stroked my head.

I agreed, and everyone helped me move what we could out of there. We saw Sirena look through her window, like a kid who had no one to play with, but I could only pray she'd understand.

A week later, my apartment manager had gotten my place straightened out. But I was still too shaken to go back home. Torian and Loni had only a two-bedroom apartment, so I was sleeping on their pull-out couch. After laying two egg crates on top of each other, the pull-out couch was quite comfortable. Also, I felt very secure around my girls. The police still had no clue as to who had broken in. I didn't know it would affect me so much. However, just the thought of someone touching my stuff, being so angry that they'd break in and destroy everything, creeped me out.

"You sure you going to be able to go to this public-service project?" Torian asked as the three of us got ready to go to the local rape-crisis center to throw a Valentine's party for the women, before the actual holiday.

"I'll be fine," I said as we headed out the door.

As soon as we got there, we saw fourteen women of various races, sizes, and ages. I became overcome with emotion as I imagined the abuse they must have suffered.

After the program loosened them up a little, the women were really able to enjoy the party. The chapter had taken money from one of our own parties to cater a very special meal. While the ladies were eating, the director gave a speech with important information so no one else would end up in the same facility.

The director, Mrs. White, said, "One in every six women will be assaulted in their lifetime. A college student is four times more likely to be assaulted. Only one in seven rapes are reported, but it's better nowadays because it used to be only one in ten rapes were reported. Seventy-three percent of rapes were committed by a person the victim knew. Rape is a crime of anger and rage."

It was just one disheartening fact after another that made

me sick to my stomach. What if it was some guy that had wrecked my apartment? What if my apartment was only the beginning? What if this person was planning to come back? This was just all crazy.

Then I saw Hayden in the corner rocking back and forth. I had never seen my chapter president so vulnerable. She was always so poised and tough.

I held my chest and walked over to her. "You . . . all right?"

"No, Malloy, I'm not all right, but clearly you aren't either." She touched my hand, and I sat next to her.

"What's wrong?"

"Last year my ex-boyfriend assaulted me right before I got into my apartment." Her eyes welled up with tears as she reflected on the incident.

Clutching my heart, I said, "Oh, my gosh, that was you? I remember an incident like that, and I was so happy to hear the guy was in jail."

"He's in jail, but still the thought of it . . . I mean, he didn't rape me, but I still feel so violated. I feel for these ladies." Hayden hung her head low.

I leaned over and gave Hayden a hug. People being cruel enough to terrorize another person was a lot. She went on to say she felt for me with my situation as well. I really appreciated her caring so deeply for others. She was a great leader.

A lady with a broken arm came over. "Being raped is a horrible thing, but there is one thing about this crisis center that makes me feel so much better, and that is people like you who take the time to come by and visit us. You are all pouring hope back into us. So we can gain back all that some horrible person took away. We're getting stronger and stronger because people like you care. No matter what you guys are going through, continue to bond with each other. You can't get through these tough times alone."

Before we could thank the lady, she just walked out. Hayden and I shared a smile after hearing her meaningful comments.

It was Founder's Day for the region, and all our big sisters agreed it was going to be a special day. Everyone in attendance at the church in Conway, Arkansas, was so excited because the National President was going to give the address. And I guess inside I was fired up, too. We had on white robes that symbolized Heavenly angels. As we sat back and thought about our founders, I was pumped to hear my mom speak.

"We have five founders," she began, holding the podium firmly, giving a strong stance. "In 1919, it was decided that an organization needed to be made up of and stand for five key principals. Each was to be remembered individually every five years. I am excited that we look back on the strengths of our beloved soror, Viola Roundtree, who represents the principle of sisterhood."

I opened up the program, which had the picture of a frail yet precious light-skinned woman. The caption read A SLAVE BABY, YET THROUGH THE MIDST OF ADVERSITY SHE CAME FORTH AND ALWAYS WANTED THE BOND WITH HER SISTERS TO BE STRONGER DAILY.

"Soror Viola," my mother continued, "came from a family that was shattered from inception. Her mother was raped by a slave owner, and no one thought she should live, but her mom prayed over it and gave birth to a beautiful child. And not just beautiful on the outside, but a woman with a huge heart. She had three birth sisters who had skin as dark as chocolate. For a long time they resented her for her fair complexion. But sisterhood meant so much to her back then, she never stopped trying to win her sisters over. She never stopped caring about the bond they shared. When she was needed, she was there, and eventually they repented from years of treating her badly. It's funny, it seems as soon as she got that fixed, she came into our sorority, and she was the one who held the sorors together. The adversity you have when you gather a group of leaders—a group of strong black women wanting to make a difference—is hard to overcome. However, Viola wouldn't let them quit. She wouldn't let them pull apart. She wouldn't let all the negative attention and jealousy get between them. She kept their eye on the prize. In her mind, the prize was their hearts, their love for each other, and their passion for wanting to do good."

I looked around the room and noticed that a lot of women's heads were low. That meant they needed to repent and knew they hadn't given as much as Soror Viola had. I couldn't just cast stones, so I dropped my head as well. Maybe that was me. Sharon wasn't even at the ceremony because she knew my mom was speaking. Though I truly believed she had ransacked my place and earlier broken my car window, I really didn't have any proof. Was the hurt, bitterness, and anger I was feeling justified?

My mother held high her white candle and said, "As I light the second candle in our second year of our five-year cycle of remembrance, I say, 'Thank you, Soror Viola

Roundtree.' May you all internally reflect on the passion of sisterhood that she cared so deeply about. Dig deeply within yourselves in wanting to be a better sister. Give more than you can; feel deep within your soul. Love like it's real."

Everyone gave my mom a standing ovation. I was so proud of her. With teary eyes I went up to her, feeling so bad for all the years I had felt left out. I could only hug her. She hugged me back. I now further understood why she had to pour herself into these ladies. In order to be good at anything, you needed somebody to lift you up, and my mom was ready to do just that.

It was Valentine's weekend, and I still wasn't back in my place. I had become quite comfortable staying with Torian and Loni. They were even trading off with me and letting me stay in their bedrooms. But I think they wanted the couch, too—something about that bedding was comfortable and special. We were taking in late movies and just having girl talk. Torian had caught the eye of a basketball player from our school, and Loni and I loved teasing her.

When I told them we should go out for dinner, they started being sneaky. I couldn't figure out why they were all giddy. Then Loni came out with my suitcase packed while Torian dragged me to the car.

As we drove, I noticed they didn't have any clothes. "So where are we going? Y'all finally kicking me out?"

"No, silly. We're going to the airport." Torian said, laughing at me.

"What is going on?" I said when Loni hushed her.

When we pulled up to the curb check-in, Kade stepped up to Torian's car with two tickets in his hand. I was so shocked.

"Now, what is this? I am not going on an overnight weekend with you—forget it. No!"

He kissed me on the cheek and said, "We've got separate rooms. For me this is business. I need your support at the NFL Combine. I need you there. I know you haven't felt right about going back to your place, so I thought you getting out and staying at a hotel for a weekend would make you feel good."

The NFL Combine was a yearly event in which the top senior college football players showed their skills before NFL scouts. It was a huge event. It was known that this event could raise the stock of players, if they did a great job, or lower their possible draft selection, if they didn't show well in each area.

"Indianapolis? You're taking me to your event?" I had forgotten it was this weekend. With studying and trying to get my nerves back, my days were all scrambled together.

He waved off my friends as Torian and Loni got in their car and left. I couldn't believe he had done all this—buying me a ticket and getting me my own room in the same hotel. I had to be there for him and show him my support.

On the plane, I said, "I don't know if I'm going to be able to stay in the hotel room by myself. I jus—"

His warm lips met mine. "You'll be fine. You're coming to help me, right? You're my big girl, right?"

"Yeah."

When we got there, I had to admit, it did feel relaxing. He had a spa retreat set up for me. I knew his agent had sent him some money, but my boy had gone all out. Ten dozen roses were in my room. They were purple and white and absolutely stunning. Kade said they were for my number when I was on line. There was a bag with all kind of Beta paraphernalia. My guy was so thoughtful.

The first night was a little rough. I kept tossing and turning and then turned on the radio and found a gospel channel with an old song by an artist named John P. Kee, one of my mom's favorites. I remembered the song, *Jesus is Real*, and if He was real, I didn't need to fear. He was the truth and the light. Nothing in darkness could keep me down.

I slept so good I didn't wake up until the ringing of phone the next day. It was Kade in a panic.

"What's wrong? What's wrong?" I asked.

"My time is off, my jump is off, my vertical wasn't good. My stock is going down, Malloy. I can't see the first round anymore from where I'm standing. You ain't watching it on ESPN?"

I flipped through the channel to ESPN, and sure enough they had the NFL Combine there. He was supposed to have been the best linebacker present, but his scores had him eighth out of twenty. The commentators were dissing his performance.

Waking up and needing to encourage him, I said, "Look, you've got to get a grip. You've got to believe in you. You went out of your way to get me out of my fear. You brought me up here to give me the chance to know that I can do it—I can be on my own again. Thanks to you, I got through last night. You're going to get a chance to do this all over again. They take the best marks. So collect your thoughts. Get yourself together, and don't just give a little. After you give one hundred percent, know that you are not through. Turn it up another notch 'cause you have more to give."

15

POWERFUL

Kade had managed to turn around his first performance and ended up impressing all the scouts. However, the second day he worked out for them, he went back into a little freeze. I didn't know if it was nerves or what, but as I sat in the hotel room and watched his performance, I could have jumped through the tube and choked him. He had it in him—I couldn't understand why he froze. And when he came to me, he was so distraught. I'll never forget him saying how bad he'd messed up our future.

I told him to calm down. We were just college students. Sure, he was about to graduate, be in the world, start his life, but I was still had a couple more years of college left. I wanted to go to New York and intern, work with some top fashion designers. Really spread my wings before I even thought about settling down. I didn't want him to put everything in me, and when I told him that, our communication just sort of shut down. We barely spoke our entire trip back.

"Okay, we're at your girls' house," he said in a bitter tone when we arrived to Torian and Loni's place.

"I know, but I was hoping maybe we could talk a little longer." I didn't want to leave him all upset over this weekend.

Reaching over and opening my car door, he said, "We've been together for five hours since I picked you up from your hotel. While we were waiting in the airport, you didn't talke to me. On the plane and in the car, you ain't said two words to me. What you need to talk about now?"

"Well, it seems you haven't said that much to me either, Kade."

"Exactly. I'm not mad at you, Malloy, but I'm needing some alone time. Let's just talk tomorrow."

Closing the door, I said, "I can't leave you like this. Everything is going to be fine with the scouts, baby."

"You read the sports section of the paper on the plane," Kade said as he grabbed the crumbled-up section from the backseat and shoved it in my face. "You think I'm supposed to be excited that my stock is slipping from being a top-five pick in this draft?"

"That could change tomorrow." I snatched the paper from him and tossed it back to the backseat.

"Money talks. The higher you are on the board, the more money goes in your pocket."

"I just hear you talking about money."

Shaking his head, he said, "That's what it takes to make it in this life."

"No, what you have to hear," I said as I pointed at his

chest through the open window, "is what it takes to be awesome in this world. You are a man with a heart of gold. Football does not make you. You are a player who plays with passion because it's inside your soul. You want to do amazing things for your mom, for us, and I was just trying to take off the pressure. At least to let you know you may not need to support me."

"Yeah, but it feels like you're saying you don't want to commit to me like that."

"No, I'm not saying that. I'm just saying you don't need to rush into anything so serious. Now, you don't need to be thinking about what I need or don't need from your finances." He had to know I was self-supportive and not with him for his potential earnings. "I want you to get all you're supposed to get. I want you to be the number-one pick because I believe you're the best player coming out of the draft, not because I want you to give me some of what you make."

"You're just so different, Malloy. I know you're a daddy's girl. I know he takes care of you. But I want to be able to do that, too."

I just reached over and kissed him. I couldn't promise him a future I wasn't sure we would have, but I certainly knew right then with all my heart and soul that I was his in every way that counted. Even as I kissed him, I could tell he didn't want to quit sulking. However, I would not let up. I caressed his face and got a small smile out of him. Then I knew he was starting to feel me. I took my hand and slid it up his chest.

"Torian and Loni aren't home. We've got this big party

tonight, and I know they're already there setting up. Why don't you come in?"

I got my bag out of the backseat. It didn't take Kade but a second to pull into an actual parking space, get out, and follow me closely behind. The brother was checking me out; I could feel his eyes on me. I used the key Torian and Loni had given me and let myself in. As soon as we got in the door, we were taking off each other's clothes. This was me giving in because it just felt right.

When I stood before him, he pulled back and said, "I . . . I can't."

"What? What do you mean, you can't?"

I was baffled. We'd been dating for months and hadn't gone there since that first night. We had now gone out of town, and though he had come to my hotel room, all he'd done was hold me all night. Now we had an opportunity to go all the way, and he was telling me he couldn't? What? No, uh-uh. I wanted him.

"I really can't explain it, Malloy. God's working on me here."

"God? Are you kidding? He knows how much I care about you."

"Sorry. I just can't. I'm asking Him to bless me, and I need to play this His way. Sorry." He kissed my brow.

So I went into the bathroom and slammed the door hard. The Almighty had given my man a conscious. Honestly I was mad.

"Come on, Malloy. Come on out," Kade said, as I sat in the bathroom trying to calm myself. If he was still wearing nothing when I opened the door, the Lord and I were going to have a real serious counseling session. The brother would just be too fine to resist.

"Babe, you don't understand—all I've been doing is kicking it with girls during college. Girl, I want you so bad. I'm tortured at night sometimes thinking about it." I heard him lean on the door. "But now I'm tryin' live to His standard. You're different than all those other girls."

I came out wearing a bath towel and said, "It's cool, whatever. Um, could you drop me off at the spot on campus where we're having our party? I know my car is out there, but this way I can ride back with my girls."

"So you're going to go out? You just got in. You aren't tired?"

"Naw," I said in a ticked-off voice.

I couldn't believe I was being such a baby about it. But I was upset. I didn't want to be turned down. I just knew he would give in, not want me to go out, and allow us to continue finishing what we started. But when I heard someone fidgeting with the front-door knob, I looked back and saw he heard it, too. Kade picked up his shirt and dashed into the bathroom.

"Hey, girl. Glad you're back. They're going to use my strobe light at the party. Why aren't you dressed—you just got out of the shower? So many men at the party, girl, we're going to have a good time," Torian said, as I put my finger to my lips. "What? What's going on?"

I pointed to the bathroom door and whispered, "My man."

"Oh, Kade's here." She laughed and then yelled, "Kade, you have to come to our party!"

"Naw, I have to get on back to Arkansas. I'm sure a lot of my teammates are down here, though."

When he came out of the bathroom, Torian smiled and tried to help play it off. "Not many men there at all. Just a few."

"Yeah, all right," he joked.

I went into Loni's bedroom and got dressed. I was not gonna miss the fun. Kade knocked, and I opened the door.

He said, "Hey, sorry if I let you down. I just want everything to be right with us next time. I don't want us having anger and animosity between us. I just need to feel it's the right thing to do. I don't know. A lot of stuff is on my mind. Maybe I shouldn't blame it all on God getting me back for being a freak, but I'm freakin' out!"

"Hey, if you want me to stay," I said, coming out into the hallway and looking at my man in the eye, "I'm here for you. I don't need to go."

"Naw, naw. Enjoy yourself." He reached out and kissed me.

Nobody at the party would be able to make me feel like he could. That was for sure. About twenty-five minutes later, I was dancing in line with my sorority sisters. All the men and women were really feeling the party.

"Ain't no party like a BGP party, cause a BGP party's got it going on! We rock, we roll, got so much soul! All the men in the place want to get in our face! Yes, it's the jam! *Beeeebop!*"

When I got off the floor, Sharon came over to me. I wanted to walk the other way. I was finally stress free, dang!

"Can I talk to you?" I really had been having a good time, and I wasn't trying to get into any kind of tiff. But then she said, "We're sisters. We do have a bond. I'm just asking for a minute of your time. You're not going to give me that?"

Huffing, I thought I couldn't refuse her request. We stepped over to the ladies' bathroom. For a long while she just she looked at me.

"What's up?" I finally said.

"I hear you think I've been destroying your property. The first time that happened to you at that gig up there at the University of Southeastern Arkansas, I did think you deserved it. I didn't do it, but I think you deserved it. But then your place being ransacked—it wasn't me. My heart hurts thinking someone would do you like that."

"Sharon, I know you're trying to put on an act because we're sorority sisters. We don't want to have any tension between us. Everybody knows or thinks you're such a good girl, but I know the real you. I know how bitter you are. But Kade is mine, and he and I have our own issues, so everything ain't precious in our world. What, you mad now because they say he's going on to the third round of the draft? You don't even know me. Talking about being sisters. Please, get out my face."

"I didn't do it." she yelled when I left her fake presence. "My love for my sorority is too strong to do something crazy like that. For real, it wasn't me."

I blew her off. She was just talking noise. She'd done it. I went back to the dance floor and started groovin' with the sorors I could trust.

It was funny because my place had been ready for a while, but I was still staying with Torian and Loni. But it was time; I wanted to get my own space back. After I helped clean up all the beer bottles, balloon pieces, and extra trash from the food we'd served at the party, I told Torian I finally was gonna get my car and my things and head back to my place.

"Girl, I just don't think you're ready."

"No, really, me staying in that hotel—it really helped."

"What? Are we driving you crazy?"

"No, no, I'm just saying I need my independence. Y'all can come stay with me some nights."

When I got to my place, the weather was a little breezy. Torian had insisted on following me over. She'd said she wanted to come because she didn't want to leave me in case I really couldn't take being there by myself. We walked in my front door and were immediately freezing.

"Why is it so cold in here? They left the air on or something?" Torian asked.

"I know right. It feels like Antarctica," I said.

She walked around me. The new paint on the walls made my place look better than it ever had. My dad had been working with the landlord to get it straight, and he'd kept asking me when I was going to move back in so he could get his money's worth

"Oh, no!" I heard Torian frantically holler.

I dashed down the hall and saw that my back door had been kicked in. I sank to the floor; I couldn't even take it. The place was immaculate. Nothing had been harmed or touched except for my door.

"Why is somebody doing this to me?" I was clearly upset.

"I'm going to check around," Torian said as she whipped

out her cell. And then I heard her say to the phone, "Y'all have to come in here. We have trouble."

"Who are you calling?"

"Sorors. We just need to make sure you're okay. And you aren't. We got to get to the bottom of this."

"What's going on? What's wrong?" I asked as Torian handed me my Beta Gamma Pi jacket.

It was torn up worse than if a dog had bitten it tons of times. Knife gashes had ripped the jacket from one end to the other. I just held my jacket and rocked back and forth. My head started hurting as if someone were kicking me in it deliberately. I didn't understand any of this.

"Sharon would never do this to our stuff," Torian said to me. "Do you think, Malloy? Really?"

"No, I don't think she did this."

Hayden, Bea, and Loni came in. They yelled out that it was them so we'd know not to fear. I was so tense, I jumped when I saw them anyway.

Loni hugged me. "Y'all, I'm scared. This is crazy."

"We got your back. We're going to report this to the police and let them come and get any evidence they can. And we're going to watch and find out what's going on here. Police can do their jobs. We're going to be in this together and make it happen," Hayden said. "Someone comes up against one of us, they're coming up against all of us. You are our sister. You will not be tortured in this way."

I moved in front of all of them. "I can't ask y'all to do that. What if whoever is doing this sees you and hurts you? This is too dangerous. No."

"You can't tell us not to care. You can't tell us we're

not going to get involved," Hayden said as she came over and put her arms around me. "Someone is messing with our sister, and they just don't know what a mistake that is. We are Beta Gamma Pi. We're too strong to be shaken. United, we're powerful."

16

BULLYING

"I'm not going to let you guys put yourself in harm's way for me," I said in a heartfelt tone to Loni, Bea, Hayden, and Torian as I stepped back from Hayden's grasp. "Yes, we're sorors, but I want it to stay that way. If anything were to happen to you guys, I just wouldn't be able to take it. So, thank you, but no, thanks. I need serious help, but I want y'all to stay out of this. Somebody's crazy, but that is my problem, not my chapter's problem."

Hayden stepped back close to me and said, "Look, I'm the chapter's president. I learned that I can't speak for everybody—that I have to take things through the proper channels—but on this particular call I will talk to everyone, including Sharon. You are not going through this alone."

"I feel so bad. I was convinced she'd done all this. All

my accusations . . . She won't be able to forgive me." I dropped my head in shame.

"Once she understands the love that one Beta has for another . . . We may get angry, we may get mad, but violence? We need each other too much. She'll forgive you." Hayden squeezed me. "And there is nothing you can say and nothing you can do to push us out of this whole thing. We're in it. Okay?"

Then my girls sat me down and took care of everything. My mom was called; the police were called; Kade was called. I was in such a trance that I heard talking, but I was out of it. Still, I could not fathom why this was happening to me.

A good bit later, Torian brought me the phone. My mom wanted to check on me, but I was half hearing what she was saying. As I let the phone drop, Torian assured her I wasn't going to be there alone and that the Betas were taking care of everything.

Moments later, my dad was kneeling by my side as Mikey and Kade stood on both sides of him. I hadn't ever seen my dad tear up. Even the day he'd pulled out of our driveway to move on without me, I remembered being the only one crying.

"Guys, she's numb," he said as he took my hand.

"She's been like this for hours," Loni said.

My dad pulled me up and sat in the spot I'd been in. Then he inched me onto his lap. I leaned on his shoulder and finally felt peace. He kept saying he loved me until I broke my trance.

"Daddy, I love you, too."

"The policeman wants to talk to you, and an emergency worker wants to check you out," Hayden said, obviously handling everything.

My father helped me to my feet. After I was cleared for just having a panic attack, I gave a statement to the same officers who had been at the scene months back when my place had been ransacked. They told us they could not believe I had had another incident. My father didn't appear thrilled that they had no leads. He stepped up to one of the detectives and said, "Listen, this is getting very serious."

"We didn't find any unfamiliar fingerprints last time. The perpetrator must have been wearing gloves."

"Well, you've got to catch him," Kade said with urgency as he came and stood next to me.

One policeman looked at the other in a strange way. "Sir, she was saying you were together here earlier. Might we ask you a few questions?"

Kade walked over to the corner with the blue suits. "Yeah, sure, I want to help you guys catch this guy."

"When she left, where did you go?"

"We weren't even over here," Kade said defensively, now understanding that the detective might be alluding to the fact that maybe he had been the one looting.

I quickly came to his side and said, "No, you're barking up the wrong tree. This is my boyfriend."

"No relationship is perfect, ma'am and sometimes it's the people you think you can trust who cause the most damage."

"Officer, I'm pretty sure it was not this young man." My father vouched for Kade. "He's my son's best friend and a dynamite football player at the University of Southeastern Arkansas."

"Wait. Oh, my goodness! You're Kade Rollins—you usually have on football gear." One of the officers got starstruck, lost focus, and asked for his autograph.

The officers then joked with Kade. Mikey walked my sorority sisters out because Hayden was insistent they head out. I told them I'd be over to their place in a bit. I stood by my dad and began shaking as I again thought about all this.

"What have I done, Daddy, that somebody would want to do this to me?" I asked.

"Honey, this is some whacked-out crazy person. It's not even what you have done to them. They're just perverted and twisted—some guy that ain't got laid in ages, I bet. Seeing you come in here all happy—he may have just snapped. You're going to get your stuff, let me put in a security system, and then you can come back. You cool staying with those Beta girls?"

All of a sudden Sirena came rushing in before I could answer. "What's going on? Malloy, girl, what's going on?"

"I'm alright, girl. Sirena, this is my dad. Dad, this is Sirena, the girl who lives next door to me."

"Nice to meet you, sir. Sorry it's under these circumstances, police cars and emergency vehicles in front of your door. What's going on?"

"Somebody broke in here again."

My dad asked, "You didn't see anyone over here did you, Sirena?"

"No, sir, I know Malloy lives alone, and I keep watch all the time. I was on campus with a study group this weekend. I wish I would have run into somebody trying to hurt her. Where's your stuff? You have to come stay with me."

"No, thank you. It's okay. I'm gonna chill at Torian and Loni's place."

"Uh-uh. That's crazy. Your stuff is right here. You're right next door. If the police have to come back and ask you any questions, you'll be right here."

"It's fine, but I'm trying to get away from all this right now," I said in a sweet voice, trying not to hurt her feelings.

"Fine, do whatever. I was trying to give you a place to stay right next door, but if you don't want to stay, cool," Sirena said, getting all upset before she exited my place huffing and puffing.

Both my dad and I just looked at each other. She was so high maintenance. I appreciated that she cared, but if things didn't go her way, she could have such a tantrum. Right now I needed her to back off. She was applying too much pressure. Couldn't she see I couldn't take any more.

My dad joked, "Stay away from that one. She's crazy."

After the police made sure the back door was secure, we left and locked the front door. My car was already loaded with stuff. The three men in my life looked pitifully at me. I knew they, too, were worried all this was happening.

My dad stood with me alone by my car. "Daddy, you do not need to get any surveillance or camera equipment for my apartment. It's going to cost a fortune," I said.

"Well, the police are not doing their job. I want to make sure my little girl is taken care of. You don't need to let nobody know we have a watch out. Nobody! Sorority sisters, Kade—*nobody!*"

"Yes, sir," I said as we walked back over to my brother and Kade before my dad took off.

When my dad was gone, Kade said, "I've got to go back, babe. Some scouts are coming to give me an individual workout tomorrow, but if you need me to be with you tonight, I'll stay."

Mikey said, "Naw, Kade. I need to get you back, if someone needs to stay with my sister, I can do that."

The two of them bickered back and forth as to who was going to take care of me. At first it was cute. Then their voices got louder.

"Why don't the two of you just follow me out of here, and when I turn into Torian and Loni's apartment, y'all can jump on the highway and get back? I'm a big girl and can take care of myself. Nothing will be accomplished with the two of y'all fussing. Remember, we're on the same team."

My brother gave me a kiss on the forehead. "I'm serious, girl. Call me or this dude if you need us."

"I'll be okay."

Kade said, "Yeah, don't let me have to hear from Sharon again that you need me."

"I can't believe Sharon called you tonight. I thought Torian or Loni did," I said as Kade held me tight. "I was out of it, though."

Holding me tighter, Kade said, "I'm just glad you're okay now. And I'm happy Sharon isn't the one doing this to you. Then another side of me is really creeped out because I just don't want you to ever be alone. I'm nervous."

"Don't worry about me. We've got Beta week coming up in two weeks, and we're training for our probate show so we can compete at the National Convention. I hope you can attend it this year," I said, remembering our pleasant rendezvous last May when I had first met him.

"Probably not, sweetpea. I'll probably have to be at someone's training camp."

"You know I enjoy being in your arms."

"Don't say that. You're making it so hard for me to leave you."

Mikey pulled us apart. "Forget the mushy stuff. All right, let's follow her out."

When I got back to Torian and Loni's place, I was so tired. I couldn't go to bed, though; the cozy place was cramped. All the chapter sorors were over. Turns out Hayden wanted to have a emergency meeting for Alpha chapter. At first I thought this would be all about me, but then I was surprised to see Keisha standing among everyone.

Torian greeted me at the door and whispered, "They were called to talk about what's happening to you. Keisha got word of us getting together and crashed our meeting. She's trying to convince us not to testify against her."

I nodded and sat down to hear what she had to say. Actually, I hadn't thought about Keisha in weeks. So much stuff had been going on since the accident. I knew she was okay; I had seen her in passing a long time ago, and I was thankful my prayer for her recovery had been answered. She wasn't even attending our school anymore, so I just assumed all was well. I had forgotten that she was going to be tried for voluntary manslaughter. She'd almost lost her life, Sharon's baby was gone, and so was the precious soror from Beta chapter. However, for Keisha it seemed like this was only the beginning of another dark period. I could tell from the looks on the girls' faces that the chapter was torn.

"I know what I did was wrong. I just always thought hazing was okay. I mean, that is how I was brought up—old-school style, you know? Make people understand that these letters, these symbols can't just be handed over." Keisha wasn't winning me over with her words.

"I understand that," Hayden said, "but a girl is gone! I asked you guys to lay off the pledges, and you got with Trisha, my girl, who is already suspended for money laundering last year from the chapter. Then y'all start to drink and get even wilder, and your actions took human life. I can't . . ." Hayden couldn't finish—she just started crying.

Sharon wasn't there. She was so upset with Keisha she couldn't face anyone yet.

"Don't y'all think I've suffered enough? I didn't even know if I was going to live and I didn't want to know what I had done, but I wasn't thinking clearly. Now I just need your help. You know I didn't mean to take somebody's life. Don't sell me out." Keisha got up and left.

Everyone was squabbling back and forth, taking different sides. Sadly our chapter was divided. Some supported Keisha's stance; some were completely against backing her in any way.

I got to my feet and hollered, "If we haven't learned anything out of all this, haven't we learned that truth can bring us closer? This is supposed to be a Christian organization. Let's stand on God's side for a change. And if we let God prevail, He'll take care of everything else."

A couple weeks had gone by, and thankfully the sorors had taken my advice. When asked to give their testimony, they told the truth. No one wanted to see Keisha go to jail, but no one wanted the two lives that had been lost not to have justice either.

I guess that was the thing us young folks had to learn—there are consequences to our actions, and being a part of a sorority, we were supposed to be our sister's keeper. Our sisterhood meant not just getting along, it meant holding each other accountable. It also meant taking a stance and helping your sister be better than she was the day before. We were supposed to get on each other's tails when we dropped the ball. I was proud we were doing that.

Because the trial was so highly publicized, we canceled Beta week, which was great for me because it was draft time and Kade insisted I come up to the football complex at his school and watch the draft with him. The draft invited only a select group of players to New York—the top five who analysts estimated would be picked first. Kade was a little upset because although he had been previously promised one of those invites, at the last minute that prestigious offer had been revoked. However, they did send an ESPN crew to his campus to broadcast the whole thing because he could go anywhere from the first round to the end of the third round.

We were on pick number ten, and he hadn't gone. There were hundreds of people, players, fans, and family who were there to support him, but he couldn't take the pressure. Upset and embarrassed, he got up and went outside. I followed him.

"It's going to be okay, you know," I said as I touched his shoulder.

"I'm embarrassed, don't you see it? After every pick they're showing me sitting there waiting on my cell to ring. No team wants me. Just because I didn't have high numbers at the NFL Combine, teams have backed off me. They're saying that because I was hurt this season that I won't go the extra mile for my team. I knew I should have gotten back in during that first game."

"Are you blaming me?" I remembered telling him during that first game that he didn't have to go back out and play.

He cupped my face. "No, no. I don't want you to misread anything I'm saying right now. You gave me your advice, and I took it. If something had gone wrong, I wouldn't even be here with a chance to be drafted, period. I'm just frustrated, that's all, baby."

"Give me your hands." He gave me his hands, and I grasped them firmly and said, "Lord, only you know if this man is going to be drafted. We put this in Your hands a long time ago, and right now we're trying to be the potter. Help us remember that we are just the clay and that what you have in store for Kade . . . Nobody can take that away. Give him the peace and confidence to rest in You this day. Whatever You may have happen, may it be joyful news for his heart and soul. We love You and thank You for this opportunity. And we tell You right now Lord, that if you see fit to give him a chance, he will continue to walk in stride to please You. He's trying. Trust me, I know he's trying."

Kade squeezed me real tight. His mom ran out and screamed, "Your cell! Your cell is ringing! Boy, come on in here and grab this phone!"

Sure enough, God had heard us. Kade was the fourteenth pick of the first round. The New York Giants had selected

Kade Wallace. Kade threw me in the air and thanked me for truly being there for him.

After much celebrating, the limousine Kade had hired for the day, dropped me back off at my apartment. Kade kissed me and told me I'd be okay staying by myself. I smiled because I could tell he was worried about his girl. However, he had to fly out to New York, and I wasn't going to keep him from his dream.

I was so happy for him. I couldn't wait to find out how he liked his new team. Now that he'd be signing with a pro team, the endorsement deal with the shoe company could be fulfilled.

As soon as I woke up from my nap, my phone rang and I quickly answered it. "Hey, baby, you got there already?"

"This is Sirena from next door. I can't believe you're home," she said angrily. "I have been watching your home, and you didn't even have the decency to let me know you were back. Then you're going to pick up the phone and answer like it was your boyfriend. You are such a slut."

Click! I hung up the phone quicker than I could think. Sirena wasn't going to steal my joy. I was so sick and tired of her. She needed to know I would not take any more of her bullying.

GONE

*n*o sooner had I hung up the telephone than Sirena came rushing over to my door and started banging on it. I wanted to tell her tail to go away. I did not want to talk to her. I did not feel like getting grilled. Dang, I was tired, but she knew I was home. And she kept banging, so, reluctantly, I opened the door, ready to stand up for myself.

Sirena surprised me by being rather pleasant. "I'm so sorry, Malloy. I shouldn't have been so pushy. I know I sounded crazy, girl."

When she tried to come in, I said, "I'm tired, Sirena."

"It's cool," she said, pushing open the door.

"I would have let you know I was back in, but I just got in the door and fell right to sleep."

"Oh, naw, naw. I—I know you would have let me know. I know you're tired. I ain't trying to hold you up. I wanna see you for a second. You gonna make me stay out here like this? I've been watching your place. You ain't gonna let me in?"

"Okay," I said, going against my better judgment and opening the steel door, locking it after she was inside.

She kept making small chitchat, talking about absolutely nothing—nothing worth listening to, anyway. I wanted to unwind in my place, to relax and chill out. It was all locked down and secure. I had just had a great day. I just wanted to take a nice, hot bath and be left alone. "I'm not trying to be rude, Sirena, but, girl, you gotta let me go to bed. I need to take a bath. I'm hot."

"Yeah, you're hot all right," she said.

I was so taken aback I stood there frozen as she rubbed her hand up and down my face. I'd been in her presence a lot of times, and she had always had a big-sister type of attitude, but I had never felt like she was trying to get with me, or I would have cut this off a long time ago.

"Hey, I don't swing that way," I said as she placed her other hand around my waist. "Get back!"

I pushed her when she would not move. She went to the kitchen and grabbed a knife. My heart stopped beating. She pushed the knife under my chin and pierced the outer layer of skin. "Listen, I'm tired of you holding out on me while you can go and give it up to that little football player boy every weekend. I've seen him prancing in and out of here at all crazy hours of the night."

First of all, I didn't know what she was talking about. And second, I couldn't believe she had been watching me like that. She lowered the knife and ripped off the top button of my blouse.

"What are you doing?" I asked her, shaking.

"I want mine. I want you right now. You teased me all year."

"Teased you how, Sirena? I've never made you think I was interested in you, and I never knew you were gay."

"After all them free dinners and stuff I made for you, you gon' try to hold out on me now? Uh-uh, girl. I want some of this."

She took my head and pushed me to my knees. With watery eyes, I screamed, "Wait . . ."

"No, I've been waiting way too long."

"No—no, I just need you to tell me why. I need some understanding. I can't just be with somebody when I have questions." I tried to say anything to get her to distracted.

"Okay. What you wanna know?"

"You say you care about me. You wanna be with me. Did you bust my window in?"

"Yeah, because I got a cousin who goes to the University of Southeastern Arkansas, and I went to the party, trying to hook up with you. I get there, and I see you all in some dude's face. I thought if I tore things apart right then and there, I wouldn't have to deal with him no more, but you still hung out with him. You still wanna be with him to this day. Don't you know that dude can't make you feel good like I can?" she said, still waving the knife in my face.

"And tearing up my place? Was that you, too?"

"Yeah, I did. I wanted you to stay over. You promised you were gonna be with me, and when your plans changed, I just got really angry. Then I go to a party, and I see you with all them other sorority girls, y'all are all close and tight up on each other. I tore up your jacket, too."

As soon as she started laughing, I took the lamp from the side table in the living room and hit her over the head. She was so strong, though, that it only angered her. She came toward me, finally turned me over, and put the knife against my throat.

"I dare you to move," she said with the most terrifying glare I'd ever seen plastered on her mean face.

I couldn't tell if it was just my wish, but then I heard a ton of sirens. Obviously it was God looking out for me because Sirena quickly got up and went over to the window and peered out. I took this moment to run and open the door. She just started cursing, and I just started praying. *Thank you, Lord; thank you, Father.* Four officers rushed in, and I pointed to Sirena, and then this guy in a dark jacket and shades came over to me and asked me if I was okay.

Catching my breath, I asked, "No, I'm quite shaken up. Who are you? How'd y'all know?"

"Your dad hired me. I'm Ronald Weaver. I have my own private-investigator service in this area. My night watchman caught this. I called the cops when he called me. We've caught your next-door neighbor looking through your stuff."

"Looking through my stuff? I don't understand."

"Well, she came in with a key a couple times."

"A key? I never gave her a key to my place."

"I guess she had one made. We didn't know you hadn't given it to her. But when we caught her smelling your personal items, we knew then that she was not your typical friend."

"I gotta call my dad. I need to talk to my father."

Mr. Weaver said, "I've already alerted him. He should be here momentarily."

"Thank you, sir," I said as I extended my hand to him.

Sirena didn't go quietly. She just started screaming and yelling my name. I sat there in the living room shaking. Mr. Weaver brought over a blanket, and that still didn't seem to help. I couldn't believe my attacker had been under my nose the whole time. Sirena was someone I had let into my inner world, and she had wanted to harm me.

Though absolutely nothing had happened, I felt so dirty. So broken. So used. I felt like a little girl who needed her father. Just at that moment, when I didn't feel I could hold it together any longer, my dad came through the door and rushed over to me.

"Baby, you all right?"

"Daddy!" I cried.

"I knew that girl next door was extreme."

"I know, Dad. I wish I could have seen it coming. I'm so glad I didn't stay with her."

"Well, right now you gon' stay with me."

"Sir, your daughter will be safe. They're taking her assailant straight to jail now, but she can get out on bond. We can have all Malloy's things out of here by morning."

"That sounds good, Ronald. As soon as the police are done with her, I'm taking Malloy home. I plan to watch my baby. Thank you for doing a great job. You saved her," my dad said as he and Mr. Weaver shook hands.

Over the last few years since my parents had separated, my dad had not been a major presence in my life. I'd been so upset with him for that, but I knew deep down I really

needed him in my life to guide me and love me and protect me. And now here he stood doing just that. Finally I
felt safe. It felt so good.

I had been getting a lot of love from my sorors. However, I wasn't in any position to talk to them now and explain all that had happened. Right now, I was secure in
my father's love. My Heavenly Father had brought my dad
into my life in a major way at just the right time.

Actually I didn't want to talk to my mom either. Rehash-
ing the creepy ordeal wasn't sitting right with my stomach.
So my dad took her through the whole thing again on the
phone. I laid back and rode to his house.

"Naw, she's all right. She's with me. I'll tell her. Your
mom said she loves you," he said once he hung up.

"Yeah, I know she does."

"You know I love you, too, although I've been missing
a lot," he said sadly. "I didn't get to see you go to your junior or senior prom. I was out of town during your high
school graduation. I'm sorry."

Giving him the last smile I could muster, I said, "You're
here now though, Daddy. Just don't go missing from my
life again."

"You can count on it. I won't," he said tenderly.

Though I knew Sirena couldn't find me, I could not sleep
at night. I would wake up in a cold sweat. My dad would
rush into my bedroom and tell me it was just a dream. I
went to school only to take my final exams and then I
went back home.

I knew the National Convention was in a couple of
weeks and that my sorors expected me to be there for step

practice. But I couldn't go. Didn't wanna go. I felt anything but sociable, and though I knew Torian and Loni would probably never speak to me again for cutting them out of my life, I just went back to the old, comfortable me. Nobody could hurt me if they weren't close.

I was home alone after my dad left for work when the doorbell rang. "Please let me in, baby. I wanna talk to you. I'm headed to mini camp."

I answered the door. I looked a hot mess. But for some reason I didn't care.

"I know I haven't called," I said in a carefree voice.

"It's all right," Kade said as he tried to stroke my face, but I stepped away. "I talked to your brother. He told me everything. Baby, I'm sorry."

"I just don't understand how I didn't know she was so crazy," I said as I sat on a couch far across the room. "And now you're about to leave. Maybe it's just best that we cut ties, too."

"I'm going to the NFL. I'm not going out of your life."

"I don't want you to feel obligated to me, Kade."

Coming over to my side, he took my hand and looked at me with a tender expression. "Malloy, I love you. Thinking about you in my future is what motivates me to excel more than I ever have. And not being able to talk to you for these last seventy-two hours drove me crazy."

"If my dad catches you over here—"

"No, no, I already talked to your father. I didn't want any bad blood there. He knows I don't have too much time to stay, so I can't get into any trouble with his daughter. He thought it was good that I come over to check on you."

"Yeah, I don't think my dad's ever taken a day from work in his life. He took off that first day I was here. I couldn't sleep that whole night that all this happened. He didn't leave my side for a full day. Just like when I had chicken pox at eight and he was there. Weird."

"Naw, it's just love. My dad's been calling me, too."

"I bet he is, now that you're signed and rich."

"I don't know if what he said was true, but he told me he didn't want a dime from me. Malloy, he said he knew he didn't deserve anything. And his biggest regret is that he didn't give me a chance to show him that being my father would have been worth it. He told me he was proud of me because I did it on my own without him," Kade said as his eyes got a little teary.

I moved closer to him. It was so interesting that I couldn't even focus on my own problems because I found myself so enthralled with what was going on with Kade. I needed to support him. I cared for him so deeply. Did I love him? No. I shook off the thought.

Being real, I told him, "If you want a relationship with your dad, don't let money stand in the way."

"What do you mean?"

"Now that you have money, don't think he just naturally wants to take it. I mean, I thought that at first, but hearing what you just said, maybe I misjudged him. It's hard to trust people. After what Sirena did to me, I don't want to trust anybody. A part of me wants to pull away from you, but I just can't."

"That's all I needed to hear." He swooped me up off my feet and took me over to the guest bedroom I was staying in. He plopped me on the bed and he said, "You know if you need me, I'm just a phone call away."

"Well, I do hope maybe I can come to New York this summer. I'd love to intern with one of the big designers."

"I'll be meeting a lot of people. If I make any connections, you know I'll put it in for my girl."

I playfully punched him in the gut. "You concentrate on football, rookie."

"I'll concentrate on us. You know, Sharon's been calling me."

I didn't know how to respond. Was she calling him because she still wanted a chance, or was she calling him to tell him what a lame girlfriend I was? Without me asking, he divulged. "They're trying to find out where you are."

"You didn't tell them, did you?"

"Naw, but you should give them a call. Those girls really care about you. They just want to make sure you're okay. We all underestimate people from time to time. I didn't know Sharon was gonna be so clingy when I tried to cut it off. But you know, it is what it is, and you move on. But those sorors of yours—even Sharon—they really look at you as a sister. This lasting-lifetime stuff . . . don't throw that away. Sometimes a heart has to get hurt just a little so it can love even deeper and stronger the next go-around."

"Okay, so look at you sounding all wise," I said as we both got up.

He wanted me to say more, but I just couldn't utter those special three words. He bent down and kissed me anyway, and then he headed out the door, and I watched him until he was gone.

PASSION

I couldn't believe my mom had made me go to the National Convention. I'd been in hide-out mode. I hadn't even seen any members of my chapter for a couple weeks. However, my mom convinced my dad that while he was on a trip, I shouldn't be alone. And who could turn down time spent in a presidential suite? With my dad on the road and Kade away at camp, having someone near me at night just made sense. I wasn't at all expecting it, though, when I answered the knock at the door and saw Torian and Loni with tears in their eyes.

"I'm sorry," were the only words that came from my mouth. "It's just been a lot."

"We care about you, girl," Loni said, making me feel horrible that I'd pulled away.

Torian said, "Yeah, your mom told us where to find you after she saw we were so broken up. Malloy, it's hard for everybody. But you've been driving us crazy not being able to see for ourselves that you're okay."

I walked away, leaving the door open as a sign for them to walk on in. But I was blown away when I turned and saw all twenty-two members of our chapter.

Hayden stepped between Torian and Loni and said, "I told you, girl, we're one. You should know that we are always here for you. I hope you know that."

I moved to the kitchenette and said, "No, it wasn't any of you guys. Y'all didn't let me down. I felt like I let you guys down because my world just got crazier. I blamed Sharon for something that somebody else did and split our chapter apart, and there's just no way to rectify that other than to pull me away from it. Maybe now you guys can be one. Maybe without me you guys can have harmony. I just don't know how to fix it all."

Hayden came over and said, "When bad things happen to you, girl, you need family. And that's what sisters are. We're supposed to be there for each other, supposed to care about each other unconditionally. I'm not saying we're gonna be perfect, not saying mistakes aren't going to be made, but you've got to at least give us the chance to kick you in the gut for your mistakes and love you out of this painful place."

I had to sit down for a second. I held my head down. I couldn't believe what I was hearing. They cared so much for me that they had had restless nights. The chapter hadn't felt whole because I wasn't around. They wanted me still to be an Alpha chapter Beta. Surely she wasn't speaking for everyone.

Sharon then came from the back of the crowd and pleasantly shocked me when she said, "You are a better match for Kade than I could ever be."

Shaking my head, I said, "No, he was your boyfriend, and I'm sorry he and I had a connection that broke all that up."

"No, girl, you don't need to be sorry. Dealing with my own hang-ups and grief, I now see you make him happy. Before, I was so focused on getting him back that I couldn't even see that I was acting crazy. I was making my own sorors even question my character when some of them thought I was capable of vandalizing your property. You had a right to assume it was me. My actions were so suspect, it could have been. I'd be lying if I said I never thought about doing something crazy to you because I felt like you were ruining my world. But the sorors prayed me through it, and they helped me see that what's mine is gonna come one day."

This was too much. I couldn't believe she was sharing this. I was blown away by her compassion.

She continued. "You helped Kade find a sense of purpose. He is so spiritual. He wants to do better so God can bless his life with you. He loves you, girl. I just wanted to say I guess if it couldn't be me, I'm glad he's with my soror." We hugged. "Now come on and get dressed and let's go on downstairs to the Greek show."

"Y'all aren't even performing because I wasn't there to help," I said, remembering that their name wasn't in the program book.

"Girl, we aren't performing because we aren't prepared. So much has distracted us. Everybody's grades are slipping. Keisha's verdict came back, and she was sentenced to ten years in jail. Despite my pleading with my uncle, as our college president he has suspended us off the yard for a year. He suspended only certain sorors last year, but he said that didn't do any good, so he was left with no choice but to kick us all off. If we don't get our act together it could be longer than a year. Plus, we're supposed to meet with your mom about our fate with the sorority and see what our punishment from Nationals is. You don't know her decision on us, do you?" Hayden asked.

"No, we haven't spoken about it. I'm sorry to hear all this. I haven't looked at the paper or watched the news in days to avoid hearing more on my story. You guys go and have fun."

Torian took my hand. "Uh-uh. We are not leaving this place without you. And you know we'd like to stay because you're in a suite!"

"*Beeeeeebop!*" everybody said in unison, including me.

It felt great to be back with my girls.

It was the big afterparty, and the Betas were throwing down all over the room. The sorors from Texas A&M had won the Greek show. They'd had this Hispanic girl in the middle of the crowd who knew how to rock it onstage, and she was dope. I had a body Kade said killed, but this girl had hips made for modeling. When it was time to jam, this chick with the sexy black, straight hair, got in the center of the floor and had all the men in the place—Qs, Alphas, Kappas, Phis—everybody looking at her.

Torian leaned into me and said, "I ain't even know we let Hispanic girls become Betas. Why they make her one?"

Flinging my hand to hush her up, I said, "Girl, don't even sound so prejudiced."

Pushing my hand down, Torian replied, "I'm just saying."

"You know brothers still like girls with that long straight hair. If it ain't blond, it needs to move like it. Most don't like our kinky stuff."

"Oh, so you hating, for real." I was actually happy I was smiling.

"Naw, I ain't hating. I forgot to tell you, but I got a man."

"What? Gimme the scoop!" I said to Torian as she smiled from ear to ear.

She giggled. "Harry London."

"Our basketball player?" I asked.

"Yeah, girl. He's a baller. I want him to handle me in all sorts of ways, you know what I'm sayin'?"

Laughing, I said, "You keeping them legs closed, right?"

"Are you keeping yours closed?" she joked back.

"Oh, see, why you all up in my business?"

"If they closed now, they 'bout to be open," Torian said mysteriously.

"What are you talking about?"

All of a sudden, somebody put their hands over my eyes. My nose took in a familiar, alluring smell I knew all too well. I turned around and felt sexy all over when I laid eyes on Kade.

"What are you doing here?" I said, right as my brother popped out from behind around him.

Mikey said, "He wouldn't let me come by myself."

Kade kissed me on the cheek and said, "Came into town for just a couple days and had to get with Mikey to try to find you."

My brother said, "Of course I didn't mind with all these honeys in the house. Who was that girl rocking the dance floor? Y'all got a Hispanic chick in the fold?"

"See?" Torian said. "Even he knows she's not supposed to be a Beta. Right, Mikey?"

"Oh, no, she's supposed to be mine!" he teased.

"You are so stupid," Torian said and hit my brother. I hit him as well. Kade stared me down. I excused us from Torian and Mikey.

"Okay, I thought you were at training camp?" I said when we stood alone in the corner.

"No, that's in July. This is mini camp. It was only a week. It's over, and though I'll be working out in New York, I came just to see you. The coaches took everything I had. I'm drained, exhausted, tired. All that. I need you to pour a little lovin' up in here. Give me somethin'. I missed you, girl." Kade leaned in and nibbled on my ear.

Hayden walked toward me and Kade and said, "We're about to do our chapter step, Malloy. Let's show everybody what Alpha chapter's got. You in?"

"Yeah, I'm in," I said, looking at my man. "I'll be right back."

"You've really found your place with these Betas, huh?" he said. "I'm so glad to see you okay."

"Yeah, they're like my sisters. You were right to tell me to try it. What we have is tight. I'm even closer to my mom because of this."

"That's good. Mikey says she's real proud of you." He slowly let go of my hand. "Go and do your thing. Your man ain't going nowhere."

I just laughed. We'd come a long way in a year. God had showed me grace by allowing us to work out after all we had been through. I was humbled, and I was thankful for another chance. We were trying to keep things right.

Before I could follow Hayden, I saw Mikey headed my way. That crazy nut was with the Hispanic girl. He hadn't wasted any time trying to get to know her. Torian was behind the two of them. I could tell she wanted to be nosy and find out whatever she could.

"Hey," I said to the girl as I extended my hand. "I'm Malloy, and right behind you there is my line sister Torian. You're our soror. Where are you from?"

"I'm from Mexico. Been in the States most of my life, though," she said as she shook my hand and squinted her eyes, wondering why I was staring.

"Sorry, I just didn't know we had more than sistahs as our sisters," I huffed, looking away, regretting I had put my foot in my mouth.

The fly girl didn't take offense, but said, "Yeah, I get that all the time. But none of the applications said say you couldn't be—"

"Oh, no, no, no. I don't have any problem with it, and neither does Torian. Right, girl?" I said as I jabbed Torian in the arm.

Mikey teased, "Well that's good because, uh, she's about to transfer to Western Smith."

"No!" Torian screamed as I quickly jabbed her again.

"Great!" I said in a phony way.

"I lost my scholarship at Texas A&M, and I qualify at Western Smith, so I'll be able to attend your school," the girl said. Your brother was telling me you guys just pledged there. As you can see, I like to party. I'll try to get with you guys tomorrow. You're gonna be here all weekend for the convention, right? I need to meet the rest of the Betas in your chapter. Because when Alyx Cruz is in the house, the house rocks!" She walked away, and my brother quickly followed.

Torian and I went to find our chapter sorors. It was hard, with so much lavender and turquoise in the place. I so missed my jacket.

Torian said, "The house is gonna fall down if that Alyx girl moves to our school."

"Don't be so insecure. You said you got a man. You know how to keep his eyes on you."

"Maybe I should go introduce her to Kade and see if you still singing that same song?"

"All right. She's cute and fly and all, but she's our soror. She ain't gon' make no waves."

I watched as my brother danced with her on the dance floor, and a whole bunch of other guys waited for their turn. Alyx Cruz was gonna add a lot of drama to our chapter. As I saw her commanding attention, I got excited she was coming. We needed her different flavor. Instantly I could envision us doing many more things, and we'd be able to reach a whole new community.

I was learning so much about the sorority. We weren't all alike. But we were very similar and had the same core values. We were all Betas, wanting to make the world, and each other, better. As I felt Alyx Cruz's sassy energy, I knew just as my sorers had found a way to like me, they would find a way to care for Alyx, too. Next semester was going to be fun.

"So, Mom, you're really gonna suspend our chapter?" I asked as she got ready for the opening ceremonies of our National Convention. "Everybody's gonna be so mad at me. I'm supposed to have inside pull. You're supposed to cut us a break because your child is in the chapter."

Putting on her Beta Gamma Pi jewelry, she said, "Sweetheart, truthfully I saved that chapter last year, hoping you'd get an opportunity to pledge, And now because of some crazy actions, someone lost their life. The chapter has to be suspended."

She'd spoken her piece, so I tried to slip away.

"And don't try to be slick about it. I heard there was a baby involved, and that's my concern. I was looking at the grades for everybody in the chapter last week, and though yours are still up, Malloy—I'm still proud of you for that—the chapter average has dwindled from a 3.6 to a 2.6, and unfortunately, from what I understand, there's also going to be sanctions from the university. So not only am I suspending them from being able to participate, they're not going to be able to live on campus. When you go against the rules, there are consequences."

"Consequences, I know. But still, they're gonna be mad at me."

"They can't be mad at you forever for actions they knew were illegal in the first place. Sometimes you gotta look within and be angry at yourself. I've seen the bond you ladies have. Before my own eyes it has gone from nothing to something is beyond powerful. I'll be talking to everybody tomorrow. We'll make sure no one leaves the suite until all hearts and minds are clear. But for now, let's get on down here to this ceremony."

My mother looked beautiful as she put on the turquoise robe with the lavender sash. She appeared so regal, so important, like a queen. I was proud of her. "Mom?"

"Yeah, honey? We gotta get down."

"I just remembered being here last year, when the last thing I'd wanted was to be a Beta. But you didn't give up on me. You told me it was going to be something that would change my life. I just wanna tell you that it has. Thank you."

"Thank you," she said as we hugged. "We've always had a bond, but now it's even stronger. We share a common goal in life. We are sisters ready to make this world a better place. I know we talked about this before, but, honey, I'm sorry Beta Gamma Pi took so much of my time."

"Mom, I'm not. I'm just thankful I can now fully understand why you spent time away. You weren't running away from me. You were running to a cause much bigger than me," I said as we shared this special moment.

Nearly an hour later, I was sitting with my chapter. My mom was giving the convention welcome address. She had the attention of over five thousand Betas. I was moved when she said, "Many of you know that my daughter became a Beta this year. It was absolutely one of the highlights of my life to be able to pin my daughter and make her a member of our precious sisterhood. She didn't want any part of this at first. There was an inward change that took place, and now she's transformed into a young lady who loves our beloved symbols. She experienced some turmoil this year when someone on campus took things further than they should, but the sorors in her chapter came to her rescue. And though they do have some things they, too, need to make a little bit better, I want to say I see the bond of sisterhood growing among you. I know this sorority has a very bright future. Sorors, keep being better women and keep on being better sisters."

I looked around and saw the smiles on so many people's faces. There was a movement in the room, a spirit in the air, a collective agreement that we were Betas. We were proud. We could achieve anything, and I sensed we all felt that sisterhood did matter. I was proud to be a part of such a strong group of women who could put aside pettiness or jealousy and not try to hold each other back from achieving greatness. We were a group of united women wanting to be a part of the solution that could make our world better. Overwhelmingly, yes, I was happy to be a Beta.

Beta Gamma Pi, Book 2:
The Way We Roll

Stephanie Perry Moore

ABOUT THIS GUIDE

The following questions are intended to
enhance your group's reading of
Beta Gamma Pi: THE WAY WE ROLL
by Stephanie Perry Moore

DISCUSSION QUESTIONS

1. Malloy Murray does not want to pledge a sorority. Do you think her mother, the National President of a sorority, understands why? Why do you feel some people are against being in sororities and fraternities?

2. Malloy is mad at her mom and seeks comfort in Kade, a guy she barely knows. Do you feel Malloy got what she deserved when she found out she went too far too fast with this young man? What are healthy ways to deal with your discouragement?

3. Malloy longs to please her mother, so she attends the rush for Beta Gamma Pi. Do you think it was a good decision for her to give Beta Gamma Pi a try? Have you ever stepped outside your comfort zone and bettered yourself because of it?

4. Malloy finds two friends, Loni and Torian. How are the girls alike, and in what ways are they different? What types of qualities do you look for in your friends, and what attributes do you bring to a friendship?

5. When Malloy, Loni and Torian decide not to participate in hazing from the big sisters, their line sisters want to haze them. Do you feel it was right or wrong of Malloy to walk away from the intense drama? What are healthier ways for new friends to come together?

6. When Kade wants another chance at a relationship with Malloy, she is torn. Do you think Malloy makes the right decision by giving Kade another try? What is a good foundation to start a relationship with?

7. Malloy's car and apartment are broken into. Do you think Malloy was justified to think Sharon, her Beta soror and Kade's ex-girlfriend, was the one behind it all? What does the concept "innocent until proven guilty" mean?

8. Because of severe hazing, there is a devastating accident. Though Malloy wasn't a part of the craziness, do you think she was right in sticking by her sorors through the trial? How can you help a person forgive himself or herself?

9. Malloy's next-door neighbor turns out to be the one stalking her. Do you think Malloy should have known the next-door neighbor was up to something? What are things to look for to make sure no one misrepresents himself or herself to you?

10. Malloy and her sisters learn lessons from a hard year. Do you think disaster can bring people together? After you make it through hard times as a group, what are things you can learn that will keep the bond tight?

Stay tuned for the next book in the series,
ACT LIKE YOU KNOW,
available in September 2009, wherever books are sold.
Until then, satisfy your Beta Gamma Pi craving with
the following excerpt from the next installment.

ENJOY!

BARRIER

"Alyx Cruz in the house. I'm a Beta Gamma Pi girl—get out the way! Alyx Cruz in the house. I'm a Beta Gamma Pi girl—I work it all day!" I chanted as I swayed my Latina hips from left to right at the National Convention's collegiate party for my beloved sorority, Beta Gamma Pi.

I wasn't trying to be funny or anything, but as a Mexican living in a black world, it was not easy. I had it going on. The looks I got from men told me they wanted to get with me, and the looks I got from girls told me they wanted to be me, or they hated me because they weren't. It wasn't my fault that I didn't have kinky hair and that mine flowed more like a white girl's. Though they couldn't see it, I felt like a true sister from my core. But most Betas felt a Spanish girl shouldn't be in a predominantly African American sorority. If they'd take time to get to know me, they'd see I was down.

However, if another one of my sorors looked at me like they wanted to snatch my letters off my chest, they were gonna be in for war—a real fight. I hated that I'd had to transfer to a new school. I'd finally gotten people to like me back in Texas, but because I'd partied just a little too much—okay, well, not just a little too much, a lot too much—my grades had suffered. I didn't understand that my poor choices would mess up my scholarship. It was a minority scholarship, for which you had to maintain a 3.0 grade point average. I'd had to find another school that would take me with my 2.6 GPA, but I'd wished I could fix my mistakes.

Now I was gonna have to start all over again winning friends. Western Smith College, my Tio Pablo's alma mater, was where I was headed. My uncle had helped my mom and me come to the United States from Mexico when I was three. He'd died when I was six, and it had been me and my mom ever since. My mom kept his degree to inspire me to do more. So I applied to Western Smith and thankfully had got enough financial assistance to be able to attend.

I couldn't get an education any other way. Most of my relatives were trying to come into the US. I had an opportunity, and I couldn't be crazy with it. I had to make sure I seized the chance. Here I was in America living the dream.

But I couldn't focus on any of that, particularly when my favorite song came on. "Hey, get 'em up, get 'em up!" I started shouting as I turned, swiveled, sashayed, and bumped into that girl Malloy I'd met an hour before.

"I am so sorry," I stuttered, taken back at seeing Malloy

with about fifteen of her chapter sisters all staring hard at me like I'd stolen their men or something.

"Oh, no, you're fine. It's perfect anyway. I was just telling my chapter sorors here about you," Malloy said.

All these girls were from the Alpha chapter at Western Smith, where my sorority was founded. For some reason the girls in this chapter really thought they were better than everybody else. I could tell by the way they looked at me that they wished I'd go and crawl under a rock. But I was on my way to their campus, and I already had my letters, so they needed to get over themselves. I looked at them, my hand on my hip and my eyes fully awake, like, "What . . . what you gon' do?"

"*Okayyy,* let's have some hugs and some love," Malloy said as she pushed me toward them.

The hugs I got from some of the girls made me want to throw up. They were so fake with it. When I got to the last few, I didn't even move to hug them. I wasn't a pledge. They could respect me or keep stepping. A few of the girls turned their noses up at me and walked off. I didn't care, because the sorors I pledged with would always be there for me when I needed sisterhood. I was ready to get to the room we were sharing and tell my sorors all about the drama-chapter chicks.

Then Malloy touched my shoulder and whispered, "Wait, please let me introduce you. Please."

Something in her gesture got to me. I didn't know her from Adam, but she was genuine. I really appreciated her wanting to make the awkwardness dissolve.

"This is my line sister Loni; our chapter president, Hayden Grant; Bea our First Vice President; and Sharon."

Those four didn't even put up our sign, which was customary when you met a new soror.

"Now, y'all, for real, you're being rude," Malloy scolded as she turned her back to me and tried to get her chapter sorors straight.

She didn't have to go defending me. I could hold my own. And they ticked me off. Shoot, they didn't want me in their chapter? Well, too doggone bad. I was coming, and what were they going to do about it?

But then, as I saw them continuously staring, I realized they were seriously feeling threatened. They didn't know me or my heart. I had to make them feel comfortable and let them know I wasn't trying to mess up their game. So I sternly joked, "Hey, I know it's tough accepting an outsider into your fold, but in my soul let me say I feel like family. I mean, I am your soror. I know a lot of Betas who aren't really excited about Spanish girls, but trust me, I don't want the spotlight, and my letters didn't come easy. I just wanted to put that out there."

Bea smiled and stuck her hand out for me to slap. I guess some people wanted to make sure I wasn't paper. When the others girls smiled as well, I knew things were looking up.

To me, more importantly than how I pledged is why I pledged. I continued: "I plan to make a difference in the community, and I love this organization. I'm a team player; just give me a chance."

All the girls finally gave me a real embrace. I didn't know where we'd go from here, but I was excited to find out.